DOPE BOY MAGIC 3

Chris Green

**Lock Down Publications and Ca$h
Presents**
Dope Boy Magic 3
A Novel by *Chris Green*

Chris Green

Lock Down Publications
P.O. Box 944
Stockbridge, Ga 30281

Visit our website @
www.lockdownpublications.com

Lock Down Publications
Like our page on Facebook: Lock Down Publications @
www.facebook.com/lockdownpublications.ldp
Cover design and layout by: **Dynasty Cover Me**
Book interior design by: **Shawn Walker**
Edited by: **Lashonda Johnson**

4

Stay Connected with Us!

Text **LOCKDOWN** to 22828 to stay up-to-date with new releases, sneak peaks, contests and more…
Thank you.

Submission Guideline.

Submit the first three chapters of your completed manuscript to ldpsubmissions@gmail.com, subject line: Your book's title. The manuscript must be in a .doc file and sent as an attachment. Document should be in Times New Roman, double spaced and in size 12 font. Also, provide your synopsis and full contact information. If sending multiple submissions, they must each be in a separate email.

Have a story but no way to send it electronically? You can still submit to LDP/Ca$h Presents. Send in the first three chapters, written or typed, of your completed manuscript to:

LDP: Submissions Dept
Po Box 944
Stockbridge, Ga 30281

DO NOT send original manuscript. Must be a duplicate.

Provide your synopsis and a cover letter containing your full contact information.

Thanks for considering LDP and Ca$h Presents.

Dedication

I'm sitting on my bed right now congratulating myself for this fourteenth book. My brothers are here in the room with me as I speak. Islam is in effect and our attitudes have been great for the past twenty-four hours. Thanks to my brother, Robert Bell *Nation*, Happy birthday kid. My brother Saddiq *Trillion Wyche* Saint *Cornelius Mouton*. Dope Boy Magic was literally thought about in the mix of building this amazing street series. My intentions were to make this novel a comedy. I wanted to bring life out of my characters and allow you to watch them grow. To show love, emotions, and feelings while living through my words. This series is my favorite. A classic that will build my new career for a bright and lucrative path. Of course, this goes for my baby, my Princess Cerenity. My mother Dolsellia. My twin D-Lo and Destiny, my family period. All my Queens. Five, World, Osama, Wild. May, Allah, reward you all. Besides that, enjoy the story, and remember that I love you all. Peace and Asalamu-laikum.

Chris Green

Prologue

Janita's words captured Tipton's breath in the center of his chest. Kimmi was picked up, and Peaches' family handed her right over to the sleazeball who created the chaos that was currently unfolding.

"Ain't no way they just gave my child to this man." He covered his face with both hands. "Where does he live, God? Cause we need to get there right now." Halo rushed and grabbed his extra pistol from under the living room couch. "It's no use, that nigga ain't going to that crib if he playing games with my daughter. He's been around my child for years. She knows him, so I'm not about to even play this game with, Rex. If he hands over my baby. He can go, and ties will be cut. If he doesn't, I'm gonna hunt his ass down and kill him," Tipton replied before jumping back on his cellphone to redial Rex's number.

"Baby, what if he really has intentions of hurting Kimmi?" Janita whispered as her eyes began to slightly tear up.

All he could do was shake his head because his wife's answer could not receive a reply at the time. The pain of Rex crossing him was a horrible day that he never expected to see. School, all the money, the friendship. It was memories of lies and mischievous ass actions. Fruitless loyalty played a role of deceit until it couldn't be contained any longer.

"Wassup, Big Dog?" Rex answered. The sound of his car music could be heard playing lightly in the background.

"Boy if you got any plans on making your next family reunion, you need to drop my daughter off, and I mean pronto," Tipton barked into the phone.

Rex laughed, before coughing off the blunt he sparked. His eyes glanced in the rearview mirror at Kimmi sleeping peacefully in the backseat. Her little love for him made it so easy to pull slime before Tipton placed the pieces together. "Calm the fuck down hoe ass nigga. You screaming all loud and shit. My niece sleep and I gotta take a shit, so I'm aggravated."

Tipton clenched his jaws looking up at Halo. "Rex, I want my daughter. I don't know what's snapped into you, but you need to think about what you doing, right now."

"I don't need to think about shit. My mind is made up, and besides, I've been watching you Tip. You're smart, eventually, you were gonna catch on, and I'm not slipping period, baby boy. After all, you decided to kill my dad. That's where you messed up. I'll make this clear because I know you're probably thinking of a way to record these special words. If you call the cops, I'll cut off her hand. If you try to find me and violate, you will never find her again."

"First of all, I don't know what the fuck you're talking about. Second, that's my child you talking about. You wouldn't have the guts to even play with me like that bitch!" Tipton's sharp words were spitting harshly through the line. "I've never played foul for this sour shit you kicking, right now. You took my friend, and family away from me Rex. Give me my daughter, and just leave. That'll make us even, cause I'm not stopping about my seed bro. I put my life on that shit."

"Don't we all put our life out there for who we love bro?" Rex said before hitting his blunt. "I'm only warning you. I love Kimmi, but if it comes down to me, I'll handle that. She ain't my child stupid. I'm sure you'll sit back and wonder what I'm speaking on tonight. The baby will stay with me until I receive five million dollars in cash from you fuck man. But I have time, I'll give you six months one payment every week. No less than two hundred, and sixty grand. I'll meet you tomorrow for a personal conversation. She's not gonna be with me, so if you cross any line. I'll have my crew chop her ass up to be added with the dogs' food for the weekend," Rex stated calmly.

Tipton was biting his bottom lip so hard that it began to lightly bleed. "You really ready to take it there with me, bro?"

"Do you wanna test me and see," Rex shot back before hanging up.

Silence filled the room, and Tipton's energy could be felt without saying a word. His jaws were clenched so tight that a large vein protruded from his forehead. Janita slowly moved over to him, letting her hand caress Tipton's cheek until his caged anger released. "Rex is gonna kill her if we move wrong, I have to wait," he explained before tears flooded down his face. Janita was speechless from the statement, all she could do was hold her man until his spirit was calm.

Halo moved toward them and placed a hand on Tipton's shoulder. "God, we ain't gonna lose her. I don't care what I have to do. Whatever it takes."

"There has to be something he wants because he's not doing this shit for no reason." Janita's hatred for Rex flowed through her tone.

"He said I killed his dad," Tipton spoke up, he wiped his face and took a seat on the living room couch.

"What you mean, God?" Halo asked confused.

Janita's facial expression looked as if she were trying to understand the same thing. Tipton thought to himself about Rex's statement. Never had he'd met this nigga father, so that was just another excuse because of his trickery. Within months he plotted the dirty ass movement and succeeded. Not only did he cross Shaggy, but he pulled nasty on Chocolate. A friend since middle school. The thought of Dejaun's words before he died wandered back through his skull. His plea's and the expression on his face when that bullet erupted. Tipton was really feeling the burden of taking his friend's life. That was a nightmare that would haunt Tipton for life.

"I don't know what he plans on doing, but I know he don't care about hurting her. I can hear it in his voice. Now I have to sit right here and see what he needs just squash the shit for Kimmi's safety." Tipton held Janita's hand while explaining what was at hand.

"Sounds like extortion. Is this about money, God?" Halo questioned with his body fuming with vengeance.

"Yeah, he wants money."

"How much does he want, baby? We can just pay him, right?"

Tipton lowered his head. "Five million." Silence filled the room once again.

Janita used her fingers to lift his chin and kissed his lips. "We're gonna get her back, Tipton. I promise, no matter what it takes, I'm

Chris Green

right here," her words calmed his spirit, but the feeling of Kimmi being taken was a hard situation to sit back and relax to.

Rex revealed his true colors, not only did he commit treason between his friends, and close ones. He was also stepping across the dangerous field of life and death when it came down to Tipton's daughter. "He's not getting away with this. I've lost too many loved ones for us to let him pull some shit like this."

"We have to find him, God. Kimmi is the little goddess of the family. I won't feel right until she's back with you."

Tipton nodded with understanding. The problem wasn't getting Rex the money. It was being sure he wouldn't pull slime after he received what he needed. More importantly, Tipton wanted to know the reason for his snake ass betrayal. After, his daughter was safely back into his arms. He would remind Rex of that same excuse before he placed a bullet between his eyes.

12

Chapter 1

The night had passed by slow with a drag of deep pain floating around Tipton's home. No one had slept and Tipton was sitting at the kitchen table, awaiting the phone call from Rex. Demon was now present prepared to risk his life for the child of his employer, but Peaches was panicking since Tipton alerted her about the status of their daughter. After he gave her the address to come over, she hadn't shut up since her ass crossed the threshold. It never mattered about Peaches' place in his life, but when it came down to her child. He couldn't be mad at the way she was responding to the problem. Janita moved passed Peaches with a slight mug before heading into the kitchen to sit with Tipton.

"She's really starting to irk my nerves. I know you want her to be aware of what's going on with, Kimmi, but this is only making everyone more depressed," she whispered into his ear.

Tipton grabbed Janita's hand lightly to ease her. "She only wants to make me feel like I'm the reason this is happening. Just let her talk," he huffed with exhaustion.

Surely, as those words escaped his lips, Peaches stepped into the kitchen with her arms folded. "So, you're really not gonna call the police, Tipton? My daughter is gone, and we're sitting here like this shit will create a different way to get her back," she cried with a face full of tears. Her lips were chapped from the boxes of Newport cigarettes she'd train smoked over the past two hours, and her eyelids were puffy red.

"It's not the time, Peaches. I already told you if we involve the cops, he might hurt Kimmi. I'm not gonna risk that and lose our child. I'm gonna get her back, trust me." Tipton rocked his foot at a quick pace. He didn't want to explode and place his hands on his child's mother, but her annoyance was starting to become unbearable for the entire house.

Halo stepped through the back patio and glanced around the room. "I called Sincere six times, God. He ain't picking up, and the workers claim that he got the product."

Tipton shook his head in disappointment. Janita couldn't help but lower her vision before speaking. "Sincere is hiding something, I can feel it. I know he's my brother, but lately, I've been getting weird messages and calls from him like he's paranoid. I don't know why."

"What do you mean paranoid?" Tipton cut his eyes with a curious expression. The attention in the room was completely on her.

Halo walked over to Janita's side and squatted down in front of her. "You gotta tell him, Janita. God deserves to know."

Tipton was instantly starting to grow heated from the indirect talk, grabbing Janita's chin, he turned her to match his eyes. "Baby, what's going on?"

The look on Tipton's face showed the seriousness, especially when Halo pushed the shit directly on the plate for everyone in the room to hear. "Sincere is saying the police questioned him, and he mentioned your name. He didn't want to tell you because he was afraid that you was going to hurt him, Tipton." She couldn't even look in his eyes. It was clear the statement needed to be mentioned sooner, not to mention that she knew before the current situations started to occur.

"Janita why didn't you tell me this?" Tipton's face wore a look of disbelief.

Tears started to come forth, and she mustered up the truth. "I didn't want you to kill him, Tipton. He's scared that you're gonna hurt me. He said that Rex called him and warned him to stay away or you're were bound to have him dead before anyone could know."

"How does Rex know about him and the police, Janita? He's not in tune with anyone dealing with our business?"

"He says that Rex has an inside worker. Someone who wants to bring you down. He's really about to try and go against you. I didn't know how serious it was until the shit Rex pulled last night," she admitted.

"This bitch knew this nigga was about to take my baby, Tipton. She's fucking lying!" Peaches' voice was shaky and filled with venom.

"Bitch you don't even know me!" Janita shouted, turning her attention back to Tipton. She grabbed his hand tighter. "I would never play with you, baby. I just didn't want you to think I was against you. I don't condone what he's doing and I'm fighting against him for the sake of this family. For the sake of your daughter. Baby, you have to believe me." The pain in Janita's eyes told him that she was telling the truth. She was always so loveable, and honest. Nothing could block Tipton's mind from seeing the bullshit in someone. She was telling the truth, and he wasn't about to create another situation until he got Kimmi back in his possession.

He kissed her and massaged her hand gently. "It's okay, I believe you, Janita. But when I catch Sincere, I'm gonna kill him in front of you for that. Are you still willing to stand by my side after that?"

Looking him straight in the eyes, Janita wiped her tears. "I'll go against this world for you. He's wrong and I will still stand beside you with every step. You're my husband, if he crossed you, he crossed me." She nodded in approval.

"Good." Tipton stood to his feet and looked at the entire room. "Demon, I need you to keep eyes on our perimeter. If we can get a vision on Rex. I want you to follow him until we get a location. I want my daughter back, and I don't need to make this nigga uncomfortable. Peaches I need you to trust me and believe that I will get our baby back. I'll fight until my last breath, I promise you that," he said while nodding to his child's mother.

"You better, Tipton." Peaches left the kitchen to get some air.

Halo waited for the word and nothing could ease his nerves at the time. Tipton's daughter was like his family, the actions of Rex was something he spotted from the beginning. His slick antics added up by the ton, and Halo began to run all the small incidents through his mind. Since Tipton came home, Rex never was a big fan of being around when a tragedy occured, but his face would appear after all the shit began to fall. He was the unseen face that no one expected to go astray, and cross Tipton out.

"God, it is kind of strange that Rex said you killed his Dad? There's only a hand full of people you've blessed. Who could he be talking about?"

Tipton pondered, but nothing was coming to his mind. "I really don't know, bro."

Halo stood next to him and tapped his shoulder. "God, think about it. None of this was happening until you took care of Vel. Rex was the same one who wanted you to deal with this guy, but when you asked him to come and stand his position during those times, he never showed. He dispersed, and when you flipped that switch, he disappeared."

Tipton nodded. "You're right, but that's impossible. Rex always told me that his dad was hardly around. That he had too much going on with his other family."

"Exactly, your family. Rex can't whip, God. You can, he murdered your plug, before we came home. He wanted to make sure you had nothing, and the secret of your father magically comes floating out after you arrive home. He wanted you to work with Vel because he could never get him around to be a father. The night of your barbeque, I walked past the bathroom and could hear Rex arguing on the phone. He told someone that chasing another nigga around for dope didn't mean shit when he wasn't being a father. Since then, he's been tweaking and Vel was handled not too long after. He's been using you, God." Halo was placing the shit together.

Tipton rubbed the side of his temple in aggravation. "That doesn't make any sense, Halo. Vel didn't know, Rex, I would've known."

"Think about it, God. If Dejuan wasn't doing all this. Rex was playing a triple cross with Skeet and Vel. The entire thing makes sense of how these people were finding our spots. He's been leading them our way."

The mega lightbulb sparked in Tipton's head forcing him to nod. "You're right. Sonya said that he told Dejuan to kill us and not touch the dread head. The dread head is Rex. He never clarified why, but I would have to ask Sonya once she returns." The sound of his phone ringing froze the entire room. Tipton picked it up quickly and answered. "I'm here."

"Wassup, Trey Songz, I see that you were prepared. Is there a way I can get you alone? I know your butt buddy is probably hounding your ass to listen. Step outside, Tip," Rex spoke calmly through the line.

Doing what he was told, Tipton raised a hand and stepped outside of his back door. "I'm alone, what is this about, Rex?"

"So anxious, huh? I thought you would've figured it out by now smart guy. I wondered on certain nights when I was younger if my dad would come home? If he would show up, and do the shit that normal fathers did? That shit meant nothing to him because his mind was wrapped into the paper flow. After I was born, I grew up hearing excuses. Worthless shit like he was working or maybe he was to busy chasing his first love, Mary."

Tipton's mother's name sent his anger button up a notch. Instead of stopping Rex. He held his tongue by placing a hand over his mouth. "This man sped back to New Orleans every year hoping for a hope and a dream of finding Mary, and it did no justice. He didn't want to bond with me because his other bitch ass son was the tool he needed to win. That's what he wanted to win. After all the time of him losing. I turn around and meet the golden ticket he craved. Tipton Devon White."

"Motherfucker you lying!" Tipton spat into the line.

"Oh, really, I think you got shit mixed up brudda brudda. Vel is my dad. I waited all my life to see what he chose over me and you fall directly in my neighborhood. I mean really like a block from my house. He talked about you so much that I nearly thought I was you, bro," Rex's voice sounded like he was about to release a tear.

"So, you plotted on me because your dad didn't love you, Rex? I'm your friend idiot. You crossed me out, and I've stood right next to you since middle school." Tipton balled up his face with a pathetic expression.

"Actually, you've stood in front of me Tip. Vel worked so hard to take you off that he allowed me to handle all I needed. You blocked my life, Tipton. The reason you're gonna lose is more than easy. I've waited to ruin all you've had since I was a little child. You moved into the wrong path. Now you're gonna feel me, bro. Do you hear what the fuck I'm saying, nigga?" Rex's statement was low and stern.

Tipton shook his head in disbelief. "I hear you, Rex, but I want my child. She has nothing to do with this fool, she only a baby."

"The first payment needs to be dropped off tomorrow. I'll text you the location, and just know that Kimmi is good. I have her and she's not gonna be found until our business is handled, Playboy. I made you feel my pain, Tipton. I took a visit and left you another gift. Hopefully, you'll understand what this shit means to me, bro. If I lose you lose," Rex whispered before hanging up.

Those nightmares of his mother's death began to skip quickly through Tipton's brain. The gunshot, the loud bang after Vel pulled the trigger. Those skin chill words, *"If I lose, you lose!"* That day was unforgettable, and the sight of his mother's fate was just explained through a phone call, Vel wanted Tipton's wrist.

His skill was surely a family secret, one that Jackson was willing to tell for the right price. The thought of Vel being Rex's father left him discombobulated. He sat around for years to reap his revenge for the scorn relations of him and Vel. Rex was playing under him without being spotted and succeeded. A message from Rika jumped across Tipton's phone screen breaking his thoughts. The word *EMERGENCY* was spelled in capital letters and his heart could sense the urgency without hearing her voice. Placing a call to her phone, he received the voicemail.

Without hesitation, Tipton made his way back into the house. Everyone's eyes shifted upon him entering, but Halo could sense from his look that shit still was sour. "Halo, I need you to come with me. Demon, stay here with Janita and Peaches. I think Rika's in trouble," he stressed before grabbing his gun from the counter.

Halo snatched up his jacket and followed behind him. Tipton wasn't sure what they were about to run into, but there were too many questions that needed to be answered, and Sleepy was the only one who could do it.

Chapter 2

The thick wind out in the vicinity of Atlanta Ga was rising by the second, and the weather was getting more belligerent. Tipton was driving through a shower of rain that began to pour down upon him leaving the crib. The signs of bad news continued to cross his mental, but he didn't want to settle on thinking negative. After Rex took away Kimmi it placed a cloud over Tipton's head. In order to gain her back, he needed all the help he could get. The car turned smoothly into Sleepy's home where his gate rested open. The rain flowed heavily over his crib, and a black cloud was passing slowly through his driveway, parking the car.

Tipton and Halo jumped out of the car and sprinted through the rain. They both reached the porch and paused before moving forward. They could see Sleepy's butler stretched awkwardly inside the doorway of his home. His silky, white shirt was painted red, and the side of his head was producing a large puddle of blood that flowed slowly away with the thick sky showers. Halo pulled his gun and Tipton followed suit removing a black silenced pistol from his waist. The thought of Rika caused his stomach to bubble, but he still didn't hesitate to lead Halo inside. Tipton's gun was pointed in case a surprise appeared from the next corner.

The loud thunderstorm looming over the home caused the lights to flicker. They trailed toward the living area where he witnessed the horrible view of Sleepy cradled inside Rika's arms. The bullet hole between his head forced Tipton to shiver and utter Rika's name. She slowly glanced up into Tipton's eyes with a distraught face. Her mumbles resembled a child who wasn't able to speak. Rika's salty tears dripped with pain over one of her best friends. Tipton bent down on his knees in front of Sleepy's body and rubbed her cheek, fighting back more tears.

She removed his hand and squeezed it tight. "What happened, Tipton? What happened to him?" Rika sniffled with a runny nose.

Halo stood behind Tipton and could see his hands beginning to shake. It was a mega punch on top of the situation that had yet to be handled.

"I don't know. How would I know, Rika?" he responded with a desperate tone.

"Tipton, nobody has the address but you. This place was designed for only you to know about. No one has Sleepy's whereabouts. Not even his family, only you." Rika's bottom lip trembled as she rocked his body lightly in her arms.

"I've never said anything to nobody, Rika. I swear, I'm trying to figure out what's going on." Tipton cracked his knuckles nervously.

"Sleepy is your dad, Tipton. He made his life this way for you. The house, the cars, it's all yours. He wanted to be sure you could handle the life of not worrying about a single thing. He took a blood test and predicted what he knew the entire time. You're his child." She pulled the papers from her back pocket and held them out to him.

Tipton opened the folded letter and scanned through the DNA paper. He couldn't even continue reading without releasing a light cry from the shocking information. He flipped the page and glanced at his birth certificate. Mary's name was bold and present along with a male's signature inside the father's slot.

"Is this his name?" Tipton gazed at Rika in search of the answer he needed.

"Yes, he signed your birth certificate and Mary eventually came out to say that you were another man's son. It nearly collapsed their relationship and Sleepy would die before he lost Mary. She kept you away and he followed you until you were old enough to move on your own. I asked Jackson to bring you to me," she admitted.

"What about, Vel? Why was he around? Who the hell is he?"

"He's your mother's demon. The one who couldn't stay away for the sake of what she had. He was cheating on your mother and had another child. That secret eventually came out and Mary's reply wasn't nice. She told him that you weren't his son. Instead of telling Vel, she kept Sleepy's affair on the hush to keep him out of harm's way. He still found her, Tipton." Rika began crying again while reminiscing about his mother. "They were scared that he would kill you."

"We have to get her out of here, God," Halo suggested after hearing the conversation.

Sitting inside the home only made them more vulnerable to become the next victim. Tipton stood and lifted Rika to her feet. She didn't want to release him, but the sight of his body deterred her soul to keep holding on.

"I gotta get you out of here, Rika. You're not safe." Tipton held her arms, his face showed the pain, but he refused to express it at that moment. The only thing he cared about was separating them from the location in order to contemplate on their next move.

"Wait!" Rika's mind started to realize that Sleepy was not coming back and it surely wasn't the time to forget about the most important rules that he'd explained to her in case something ever happened.

She moved over to the bookcase, removed one from the shelf and opened the front cover. Rika removed the small USB device and placed it into her pocket, then she picked up Sleepy's Apple MacBook. Tipton and Halo led her toward the front door. The sight of everyone dying gave him the feeling of Rex's nasty ass smile in the back of his head. It was clear that he didn't know what was about to occur, but even if it cost his life. Tipton was about to ensure the safety of his family. After Rika was led outside to the car. They all climbed in and pulled away from the residence with a dead silence aura. The feeling of losing another piece was unbearable. It solidified what Tipton needed to do, murdering Rex was going to be the first.

Chris Green

Chapter 3

Rex stepped out the front door of his secluded hideout and glanced out at the car pulling inside his driveway. Once the small Impala came to a stop in front of his premises. He watched as Detective Sandra Elliot stepped out with a small piece of paper in hand.

As she moved up to him, she smirked. "Is there a shortage on that phone of yours? I'm not satisfied when my calls go unanswered. I suppose since I'm here, you've come up with our agreement?"

Rex smiled with a wink. "It damn sho' ain't to bend that tushy over my bed. So, I'm quite sure it's a reason you're standing in front of me." He pulled two thick envelopes from his back pockets and placed them in her hand.

"Is this half?" Detective Sandra Elliot skimmed through the envelopes with a suspicious eye.

"Don't flatter yourself, Ricki Lake. I ain't gotta slime you when I'm the one placing this shit together. You'll get the other fifty when the job is done. I need to spread my wings, that can't happen with him around. I'm sure if you didn't have my witness, this case would probably be getting flushed within an hour of you slapping it on the judge's desk. All you have to do is handle your end, that'll be two motherfuckers happy with a huge payday." Rex flashed a crooked smirk.

"I hear ya big-timer, but I'm going to let you know a little some-some, too. If I feel you're backing out with the agreed price, I'll flip the scene of this mystery to a *Most Wanted* poster before your ass can blink. If you keep the deal coming, you're just a blind mouse to me, kid," Detective Sandra Elliot mentioned before getting in her car and burning rubber in Rex's front lot.

He flicked her the middle finger with a smile. Rex retreated inside the crib and locked eyes with Kimmi. "Wassup, Uncle's baby? How did you sleep?"

"You're not my uncle," her little voice spoke clearly.

Her arms were folded and her pupils beamed directly at him with no fear. Rex laughed at her arrogance, she looked just like Tipton. So, her heart musta felt like a Ford truck.

Rex sat down across from her, sparked his rolled blunt and exhaled directly in her face. "Guess what, Kimmi? I don't give a fuck if you want me to be your uncle or not. This is business, I could've let you starve and die when your bitch ass daddy sat in prison crying about you. All that shit I bought didn't mean shit to you?"

Kimmi's eyebrows forced the best frown possible and her chest heaved before she started to cry. "I want, my daddyyy!"

"I said fuck yo', daddy. He ain't coming to get you because he running the streets, Kimmi. He doesn't love you and that's honesty for yo' ass. Sit back and watch the damn cartoons, cause Uncle Rex won't hesitate to set you inside the stove like my mama tried to do me," he threatened with wide eyes.

Kimmi pulled her little legs against her chest. Her back was against the couch, and her eyelids didn't close until Rex stood up. "After your daddy feels my wrath. You're gonna wish I was the one fucking your stanking ass momma." He grinned with a wide smile.

***

Atlanta Witness Protection Unit

Sincere squeezed the filter of his smoked cigarette between his fingers while waiting for the officers to return for a file questioning. After giving all the details about Tipton's operation. He began begging for the best protection possible. The guilt was eating harder than he could bear and nothing would convince him to go back. All Sincere wanted was a ticket out of state to ditch Atlanta and enough connection to leave the country if Tipton became a major problem. The snitching couldn't be erased and most of his people would cut ties since they got word on him speaking with the police. It was too late to turn back. A tall, bald officer entered the office and closed the door behind him. His suit was extra crispy, and he was waiting to take a seat as if he needed permission. Before Sincere could open his mouth.

The officer raised a finger. "I only have one question for you, Sincere. Where is White's residence? This deal cannot be complete if we don't have him in our custody." He gave Sincere a non-caring shrug.

The feeling of snitching on Tipton was hard but giving him up to be arrested was even more critical. Sincere's heart thumped and he truly didn't know what to say. "H-how soon can I leave if I do this? I need to be far away, he'll kill me if this shit hits the fan." He sweated with a petrified expression. "I need to know that I'll make it away."

"Calm down because panicking isn't an option, sir. We need him locked away if you're saying he's gonna harm you. The only way I can do that is to give Detective Witherspoon a few addresses to hunt him down before you're released."

Nodding in compliance, Sincere grabbed the piece of paper and pen that rested in front of him. He jotted down Tipton's information and pushed it toward the officer hastily. "You tell these motherfuckers I want to be out of here by tonight. My part is done," Sincere demanded, his face was trying to digest what he'd done but his mind stressed freedom. Prison wasn't the route he wanted, all his incorrect decisions counted on this one big moment. Tipton was gonna have to accept his fall and respect the game.

"I'm sure the lead detective will have you situated after the papers are finalized. I have to process this and you just have to remember son. Your testimony is the only way you're walking completely away from this. This is going to be one of the best moves for yourself, Sincere. You're about to help bring down one of the biggest movements in Atlanta. That's being a true Hero if you ask me." The officer was dishing the mind games and Sincere was not aware of how easily he just signed his life away when their hands locked to seal the deal. It was a day of disloyalty, one that he could never forget.

***

Before the nightfall could engulf the sky, Halo sat on the front porch of Tipton's home and gazed out at the sun. Sonya's car pulling into the driveway caused him to stiffen his hand was already gripping the handle of his weapon. Once she protruded from the whip, Halo relaxed and continued to watch the sunset. Sonya's thin spaghetti strap Gucci dress clawed at her skin with every strut she took. Her six-inch heels were only more appearance for the creeping she had been doing since receiving Tipton's phone call the night before. Out of all the bosses in the city she connected with, none could get the gossip about Rex taking Kimmi. The only word floating was the Louie Gang members stressing Rex as their new enforcer. Nobody knew about the kidnapping issue, so it didn't feel like the right thing for Sonya to do when shit could flip with one slip.

Taking a seat next to Halo, Sonya leaned over to peck his lips. "I moved around and found nothing. All I know is Rex played smart with his little flunkie workers. People's lips are sealed tighter than spider coochie. So, I think Tipton needs to rethink how he comes at this." She crossed her legs and exhaled.

"I know, Goddess. We found some things today but it didn't do anything besides add on to his pressure."

Sonya could feel his disappointment about not receiving any new leads to help them find Tipton's princess. His daughter was an angel and the search wouldn't stop until they brought her home safely. "The only thing he can do is wait for the open opportunity. It's gonna seem sticky at first but once he finds out what's really occurring, he'll gain victory. I know how dedicated you are to helping him and it keeps his attention grounded Halo." Sonya rubbed his babyface cheek with a light touch.

"I'll never turn my back on, God. His love is genuine for everybody. He's the first person I've ever met to take care of anyone who crossed his path. He deserves to be respected and blessed for his great actions. That's my reason for rocking in this forever, God needs me," Halo said as he stared up at the sun reclining below the horizon.

"You're a real one for doing that because as you can see, not too many friends remain close. I know my boundaries with speaking any opinions but Tipton has to focus and regain his zone. He can't think if his emotions outweigh the problem. I want this little girl back just as bad as you do." Sonya rose from her chair and straddled Halo's lap. "Remember that you got a friend in me." She beamed down into his blue pupils.

He gazed at her beauty like always, she was a stonecold baddie. Every second that Halo held Sonya, he felt that solid love power connecting through his body. He grabbed a hand full of her bubble backside and his lips attached to her neck. Her melon breasts jiggled loosely in the slip overdress and her ass slowly gyrated against his manhood.

"You got a friend in me was on Toy Story Goddess. You could've done better." He smiled and rubbed a finger down her pussy.

Sonya reached beneath her and loosened his belt, pulling his hammer out. She took her time and climbed on top of it. "Ssss, Haloo!" Her face squinted when he grabbed ahold of her waist. Sonya raised the dress over her juicy ass to get a view of Halo's monster sliding inside. Her walls were warm and creamy, the sounds began to slowly rise when Sonya allowed him to dig deeper. "Daddyyy!" she moaned lightly.

Halo lifted her round booty to make sure she could meet every inch as he placed his arms under her legs. Halo forced her to get up in a squatting position. The cool slide and pump ride was nice but now his dick was hitting the spot. Sonya's ass bounced uncontrollably on Halo's rod like it had a mind of its own. She was sure to rise to the top and come down heavy like a good freak is supposed to. Halo began sucking one of her breasts while she rode that dick. Her orgasm formed once he slowed down to dig in the pussy with a few deep strokes. Sonya could feel a wet puddle erupt from her kitty down his stiff piece. The button for her sticky cum was twirling and the sight of it enticed Halo to make it talk back while she dropped her apple bottom repeatedly on his hypnotizing piece. Halo prepared to bust because Sonya was being sure to throw it back with every pump. The sound of her butt clapping loudly on top of him caused her to release a warm trail of cum down his length, he was so deep. The feeling of his strong hands taming all that ass forced Sonya to moan in delight for her good dosage.

"Here it comes, baby," Her voice was light and weak.

Halo lifted her and placed her inside the chair. Her back laid flat and the bottom of her ass hung freely off the edge. He could tell by the way her warm box pulsated that his night would be far from over. The porch was an easy place to get caught slamming all the meat into your chick but Halo couldn't help but take advantage. As he slid deeply into her slippery cooch, Halo's lips curled before he started long stroke her with his rod. Her juices shifted and farted with every pump he caved between her legs.

"Beat this shit." Sonya's eyes rolled in satisfaction.

Halo grabbed her waist, hitting the pussy harder for the massive orgasm he felt approaching. The sight of him sliding balls deep forced his manhood to erupt violently inside her guts. He could feel her muscles tighten with every drop he spilled. As they shared a freaky tongue kiss, Halo dipped inside one last time before pulling out of the warm goodies and lowering Sonya's dress. He fixed the zipper on his jeans, then sat down to catch his next wind.

Sonya leaned over with another kiss. "Thank you, baby. I love every second you touch me." Her eyes glowed with satisfaction and love.

Nothing could compare to Halo, especially the way he put that dick on the pussy. He didn't play when it came to pleasing her, and every time she allowed him to have his way. He turned the energy button up a notch.

"I'm here for much more, Goddess." He cupped her chin with a soft grasp.

"I believe you, Halo. Let's just help get Kimmi back, then see where it leads us, I'll be inside." She smiled before departing into Tipton's front door.

Chuckling from the small X-rated scene Sonya had just placed upon him. Halo sat back and tried to relax his mind. Even though Sonya knew how to change his mood. Tipton's daughter continued to pop inside his head, getting her back was gonna take more than just a conversation. Rex needed to be stopped, and Halo was itching for the chance. The waiting game was now ticking.

Chapter 4

Janita yawned lightly before cracking her eyes. She was cuddled in the bed with Tipton and judging from her huge bare ass that hung from under the covers, they'd obviously had a session of stress sex. Tipton snored lightly and the sun glistened brighter than the dark ass gloomy day before. Janita wrapped up inside of her robe, opened their bedroom door, and headed downstairs to the kitchen. The schedule was going to be nonstop in order to gain Kimmi and sleeping wasn't about to make anything progress. As she reached downstairs, the sight of numerous black SUVs was sliding in their driveway. The thought of coffee drained from her mind when she witnessed the authorities jumping out with their guns to surround the house. Janita took off back up the stairs, nearly falling trying to reach Tipton.

After busting through the bedroom door, her voice was able to wake him out of the small slumber. "Tipton, the cops are here! Their outside." She waved her hand around nervously.

The speed of flash slung under his feet forcing him to rush from the bed. "How many did you see?" He panicked while shuffling inside of their closet.

"About six to seven trucks." Janita's fingers shook uncontrollably when Tipton handed her five kilos.

"Flush it, Janita!" he whispered before the loud bang erupted on their front door.

He watched her run for the bathroom, then Tipton stepped out into the hallway and motioned for Halo to close his room door.

"Who is it, God?" he whispered.

"Police." Tipton held up a hand. "Just stay in the room, I know they want me. Don't answer any questions until I get you a lawyer," Tipton said before making his way downstairs.

Before he could open the front door. It was kicked off the hinges and bombrushed by ten federal agents. Their weapons were raised and the first officer screamed to ensure that Tipton didn't make the wrong move. "Get the fuck down motherfucker, or I'll blow you away!"

Following instructions, he got on the hardwood floor and placed his hands behind him. Two men quickly restrained him with a pair of cuffs and forced him to sit up.

Numerous men with badges flooded his home, wasting wasted no time spreading out for the search. Detective Sandra Elliot entered his threshold with a warrant held high in the air. "Mr. White, I've been looking everywhere for you." She bent down in front of him with a wicked smile.

"You're raiding my house with no probable cause. I would like to call my lawyers," Tipton requested as the agents escorted Halo and Janita downstairs in cuffs.

"Oh, I have everything I need White. I admit you had me fooled, but not for long. This little business of yours comes to an end today," she said before stopping one of her men. "Johnson, I need this place searched from top to bottom, right now. Don't miss a spot."

"Yes, ma'am," he obliged her command.

Tipton forced a smile and shook his head. "You've made a big mistake detective. My lawyers will make sure you can't work anywhere else, except behind a cafeteria's lunch line when I pay this minor problem to go away. It's not a mystery that you're standing here in front of me, right now. I know more than you think, Detective," Tipton lied to get under her skin.

Her face tightened from his comment. "You don't know anything, White. You're about to be heading down to a prison cell so fast your gonna have to share a bunk. Sincere wanted me to tell you that he's sorry," Detective Sandra Elliot whispered low enough for just him to hear.

"I know, he called last night and filled me in on your arrival. If you don't mind, I would like to get down to the station so I can bond my family out on whatever bogus charges you're about to form together."

"Ms. Elliott," the agent she spoke to a few minutes ago reappeared with a hand full of plastic wrappings.

Tipton knew that it was the same weight he'd given to Janita. She flushed everything besides the plastic which was enough evidence to arrest him.

Sandra Elliot used her gloves to place the evidence inside a brown paper bag. "Looks like someone tried to flush a bunch of illegal shit?" She grinned from ear to ear. "Take all of them down!"

"You're gonna have to come harder than that, Detective," Tipton said calmly as the arresting officers escorted him outside.

Janita and Halo were placed in separate cars and arrested until the county decided further. Peaches recently left the night before giving her a pass, and Demon was out in pursuit of his own serious task. The crib was flipped upside down and Detective Sandra Elliot was sure to have Tipton's safe cracked for proper procedures in case more illegal drugs were being stashed. The clean sweep still didn't produce another crumb. The home was clear, the only evidence she possessed was the cocaine residue wrappings.

She grabbed her radio from the waistline. She channeled Agent Witherspoon. "The suspect is in custody."

"Roger that Elliot, we're waiting for you," he responded.

Walking out of the home, she headed for her cruiser. "Shut the house down and clear it out," Detective Sandra Elliot ordered to the moving officers before getting in her vehicle to leave.

***

The Atlanta Investigation Unit

After waiting in the interrogation room for over three hours. Tipton began to grow aggravated. The small camera sitting in the corner was beaming down on his head harder than a magnifying glass over a small ant. His bad timing with relocating placed him under a radar. One that he couldn't dodge in time before the sneaky ass pigs came crashing in. Watching Agent Witherspoon enter the room.

Tipton sat up straight. "I've been here for over three hours and I need to be sure my lawyer is on the way to assist with this problem."

Agent Witherspoon ignored his remark and took a seat at the steel table. "It's finally good to meet you, Tipton."

Flashing him a mug, Tipton eyed the agent as if he had the wrong person. "How the fuck do you know my name? And how long will this chat be? I have places to be, sir."

"Let me introduce myself, the name's, Kenny Quick." Agent Witherspoon grinned before smoothing his silky hair back.

Tipton cleared his throat and chuckled. "That's a very nice name. Is it Cuban?"

"No, it's definitely American made."

"To be honest, I truly don't have time to play your game, sir. If you don't mind, I would like to get my call please," Tipton requested again.

"Mr. White, we are charging you with conspiracy and possession with intent to distribute. The evidence we discovered in your home earlier is enough to get a five-year plea from a judge. I think you need to slow down and let me explain what we're looking at." The officer held his hands slightly in the air hoping that Tipton complied.

"What do you want from me?" He folded his arms, before leaning back into the metal chair.

"First, I need you to know that we've been tracing you for months now. Sincere was caught with a lot of drugs and the only person he had to blame was you. True, we haven't caught you with anything. But your friend's testimony including our evidence against you. It'll be over within a few days into your trail."

"Bullshit, my lawyer is wiping that weak ass evidence off the stand. Your snitch ass witness has never touched anything from my hands and I haven't been involved with those types of things since I was a teenager, sir. No disrespect officer, but my wife's art gallery, including our clothing store is probably worth more than everything in your small ass possession. I bust my ass like any other citizen out there, and I ain't hearing shit unless it's my lawyer cutting the check for me, and my family's bond."

The officer tapped his pen across the table with a repetitive rhythm. His posture said that Tipton was totally confused about how shit was about work. Folding his folder, he stood up and smirked. "I'm gonna show you exactly why this is serious, Mr. White." He stood to open the office door and waved for someone to enter. After a few seconds of the Agent standing, Tipton's lawyer walked inside the small room with his briefcase in hand.

Agent Witherspoon tapped his lawyer's shoulder. "Mr. Wallace, we will need this visit to be quick. It's about time to process this," he mentioned before leaving the two alone.

Tipton sat up with a huge smile. "I'm glad to see you, I didn't think you would be able to make it."

"I came when I got the call. Did you say anything to anyone?" Wallace questioned while opening his case.

"Nah."

"Good, I've viewed the file. We have good news and bad news. Which one do you want first?"

"What do you mean good news, bad news? That sounds like it's a problem." Tipton asked curiously.

Wallace took a seat and exhaled before continuing, "It looks like you have a sale case on your hands. I've gotten a bond for your wife and friend. They should be processed out in a few hours."

"What about me?" Tipton asked before he could continue.

"Uh, that's the problem, Tipton. You were caught with five kilo wrappings inside your bathroom during the raid. The witness is active and they are prepared to build a case on you, right now. I wasn't expecting to run into something so serious. So, I'm going to start preparing your defense."

"What do you mean defense? You saying, I can't get out?" Tipton tilted his head as if he was waiting for the wrong answer to slip out of Wallace's mouth.

"Unfortunately, that is what I'm saying. These people have one of your closest associates under close watch in order to see this case go all the way. I can easily attack him, but his statements hold a lot on that stand. They want you in court, Tipton. It was either all of you or just you alone. That's how I was able to make bail on their names. You're looking at prison time no matter how the courts turn out. I just want you to be prepared for this because it's a possibility

33

that we could slip if Sincere's testimony reaches the jury." Wallace folded his hands with a look of needed advice.

Tipton sat quietly and calmly counted inside his mind. The reality of leaving out of the police station was little to none and the situation with his precious baby was still at risk. The time for authorities wasn't needed and from the looks of the way shit was flowing. Tipton was gonna have to prepare for the worst and try to compromise with Rex to quickly snatch Kimmi back. The delay was surely gonna send the radars buzzing, he didn't need Rex questioning if he was about to pull some slick shit.

"So, what am I looking at?" he asked Wallace with a straight face.

The lawyer shuffled through a few papers and huffed. "If it comes down to jail time, you're looking at anywhere from ten to fifteen years to the door. If you cooperate and we plead out to a small possession with intent to distribute. I'll ask for three years, where you serve one in the federal facility. They're trying to knock you with thirty if we lose and that's not sweet time in the city of Atlanta."

Tipton held back his anger and nodded. It was no fighting when the opposition had the advantage. "Hire me two more lawyers to work with you. Tell my wife I love her and tell Halo he has to step up. We're gonna stall these motherfuckers out until they let me go. I'm not settling until I know it's over," Tipton ordered. "Mr, White, that could end bad if we wait too long. They're not gonna stop trial and offer you anything. You gotta think right now." Wallace sat back with a skeptical face.

"Just like I said, we stalling out until I say it's over. Handle what I said and file for my speedy trial. I'm not bowing down to shit. They didn't catch me with nothing, Wallace. Sincere's statement doesn't mean shit if they have no evidence of me doing anything with him. I'm not about to be railed by the system. We can win, I need you to fix this, Wallace," Tipton requested with a calm tone.

"Okay, you're right. We're gonna take care of it. I'm not letting you down, Tipton." Wallace pointed at him with a straight face. "I'll get what you need handled and after you're ready to proceed, we'll flood the courtroom and embarrass whatever the district attorney's hiding."

"Wallace, I need you to get me a phone call. I need to speak with Halo when he gets released.

"I'll get it done, just give me a few days to dissect this and the games will begin." Wallace grabbed his briefcase and nodded to Tipton.

The tables had turned and shit twisted within seconds. Prison was the last thing he wanted to see and nothing could change that condition. Kimmi's face flashed in his mind forcing Tipton to bite down on his jawbone. His baby needed him and Rex the man who he would call on at times like these held a horrible hand of dirty aces. The hand was dealt, he knew Rex's ties with their family was the reason he wouldn't quit. He wanted everything down to Tipton's soul. The point of reality and acceptance caused his tension to release with a light sigh. There was only one plan left to place in effect. It was the final move, the time for multiple chances was about to end. Tipton knew he couldn't fail, it was his last shot.

Chapter 5
7:46 p.m.

Janita moved around the house as if she was going to die at any second. The news of Tipton being taken into custody wasn't sitting well, that including her mischievous, snake ass brother who was trying to keep Tipton behind a cell for eternity. It was a bundle of hate, and pain that she couldn't control.

Halo, Sonya, and Demon stood in the living room of Tipton's home pondering on the next move. Shit didn't go unless Tipton said so and nobody wanted to step up and call the wrong play. Any false action could get Kimmi murdered, and the movements would surely have to be more discreet being that Tipton was booked. Them folks were watching, so slipping didn't exist in anyone's vocabulary.

Halo grabbed Janita's hand lightly to calm her. "I know you're probably mad, Goddess, but you need to remain firm for God. I'm not about to let anything happen to you." His blue pupils were making direct contact.

Janita took a deep breath and grew silent for a few seconds. "It hurts, Halo. I don't know what to do without him. How are we gonna get Kimmi if he's in jail?" Her face was wearing worry and Halo couldn't answer all her questions at one time.

"Janita, I need you to remain calm. You're in charge. So, I need you to be thinking on the same page as me. Tipton is only locked up, for now, he's coming home. We gotta focus, get Kimmi and get God back home to us. You need to be right here beside me," Halo reassured Janita.

The promise of getting Kimmi home was a risky job to uphold. The crazy shit that was going on wasn't normal. It just didn't sit right in Halo's mind. Rex was moving like a real serpent with his stunts and that shit was about to come to an end.

"I'm beside you, I'll stand no matter what it takes." Janita exhaled and regained her form of empowerment. Halo was right. It would take a straight-headed person to follow Tipton's footsteps and handle business accordingly with no mistakes.

Sonya stood from the couch and paced around in a few circles. Her mind wasn't prepared to witness the shit that was going on with Tipton's child and condition. Vel created a path of terror and lots of individuals trailed because of the history with his behavior. Rex was born before Mary even had a chance to leave New Orleans. Sleepy supplied the weight and Vel wouldn't hesitate to make the trip for Atlanta. In his mind, it was the city of opportunity. Tipton moved through his life not aware of the poisonous demons that laid directly under his feet. Rex was more than just a scarred kid. He was out for relief. The only thing that eased pain was blood, and Rex was the leader of their food chain. The Louie Gang love was passed down through generations and Tipton happened to be the life that Rex had on his list.

"We need to start looking for every spot a Louie member kick it. Lock these locations down and press their weak ass one by one until we get the right squealer. Ever since Vel died, Rex been calling shots with these dudes. They all down to kill, but it's more to the story than that." Sonya walked over to Janita and exhaled. "In the mix of us making this happen. You need to make Rex more than comfortable until the right opportunity presents itself. He's probably good with sensing energy so you shouldn't alert him to the point where he gets suspicious."

"Rex knows me, Sonya. I've never interacted with him, he's beyond good with feeling vibes. He's quick to throw a joke in the air when some shit be going down. At least until he knows everybody is calmed down. He would break the ice and push on as if shit didn't happen."

"That's what we already know, Janita. The point is knowing the things Rex isn't capable of withstanding, a woman perhaps." Sonya raised her eyebrow.

"I'm never gonna act like I'm digging that dirty ass bum to make him feel better. This ain't no wife swap. Rex is trying to ruin whatever he touches, but that's not about to boost me to be this fuck nigga's woman. It's not about to work."

"Yes, it will," Sonya corrected her.

"No, it won't." Halo stepped in. "Goddess is, right. From what Tipton told me. Rex has been around him since the beginning of his first venture, down to the last. Not only did he watch Tipton for inspiration, he soaked in the art of his hustle. He's playing raw because he knows Tipton won't make a stupid move when it involved Kimmi's life. It was a form of control to get what he needs and move freely around Tipton as if they attended a family reunion the day before. He's playing a real monopoly board. One of the Louie gangs motto is to, *"Play life like it's monopoly."*

Halo bent his index fingers. "The weird part is the shit he's doing actually coincides with the board game. He sent God to jail, after cleaning the funds from all his connections. After that, he kills them and observes who could possibly be next in line. He started off with Shaggy. He continued and finessed his way inside all the spots to know how it's getting pushed. What all will be needed to take it all, and how would he play if off without being placed under the spotlight. Rex manipulated Tipton into controlling his entire life because he possessed the right keys. It's no option when it comes to the blood, being shed because we know how bad this could be tearing God down."

Demon lifted a finger before walking into the middle of everyone. "If Rex served a purpose, he would've acted and simply killed Kimmi without a dollar being needed at all. The pain that everyone speaks on lives inside him because he was raised in a household where it was just normal. His message is more misunderstood I should say."

"Well, you need to break that down cause we ain't been through college and learned doctor lingo 101. Can we just get the normal version." Sonya frowned impatient.

Demon smirked. "If you give him the things he wants. He's not going to expect your gesture. It eventually invites him towards you, and he would be willing to do whatever in order to have it. How do you calm a small child if they are being extremely disobedient?"

"Easy, whoop they ass." Sonya smacked her teeth.

"No, you ignore them." Janita folded her arms.

"Exactly." Demon grinned. "He wants attention, but if you deliver what he demands and show them no attention with their trickery and antics, the effort deteriorates. If we all think before we act and help each other. The child will easily fall back into your arms."

"That sounds good and all, but when will that be? This has been going on for days, and it's been enough time wasted when Tipton was out here with us." Sonya held up her hands with a frustrated tone. "That boy ain't playing. You still have to remember that there's a select few who stomp on this earth that just don't give a fuck. We need to apply pressure and catch his rookie ass slipping, it's easy."

"You got a point, but God already explained what Rex said about not trying to search or call the police. He's really gonna have a reason to hurt the baby if we do that. We also can go for the smooth way, and cripple him day by day. It'll guarantee us victory when all of our minds become set to move at once," Halo explained with a positive aura rising from him.

Janita didn't know if it was just the talk, but the words were tugging deep. It was truly for the man she married. To be strategic when it came down to life or death matters and stand whether the head was present or not.

"We're all in because this ain't working without everyone's help. It's for the child, not us." Sonya stamped her position.

"I'm in too." Janita shrugged without a care.

Halo and Demon nodded to each other and started to place their plan in motion. The sound of Tipton's front door opening stopped everyone's movements until Rika appeared around the corner.

"Uh, where's Tipton?"

Halo shook his head and motioned for her to take a seat. Finding her a spot at the kitchen table. She listened as Halo continued the conversation. "Unfortunately, Tipton was arrested today and they're not trying to give him a bond. There's a lot that has to happen, so we need to focus and contain that energy for when we really need it.

Rika lowered her head with a frown forming down her face. Tipton being in jail meant that her entire objective was about to be paused if she couldn't meet the limit of what he could push without breaking a sweat. He was all she had left to remember Sleepy. All she wanted to do was be in his presence at that moment.

"I know you might not like that Rika, but it won't be for long." Halo stopped her doubts out the gate and if she continued to place her business between Tipton's crew. The numbers would surely remain to drop on the correct date and time.

Rika could feel the energy of someone watching her heavy. She glanced over at Janita. The look she gave Rika spoke a thousand words without having to open her mouth at all. It was the same look she received when Tipton allowed her to stay with them until everything with her living arrangements, and business was straight. Even though she cared deeply for him. Rika refused to be somewhere that she wasn't wanted. The reason for bearing patience is because of Tipton's position.

He didn't know, but Rika refused to operate another deal unless his approval stamped it. Things were like a breath of fresh air with him because he didn't just show you improvement, he taught it. He was built to run whatever the family tree placed inside the pot. It was Tipton's dependability that made him grasp on too anybody's path he crossed. He wasn't arrogant, nor was he overbearing, just precise. Tipton didn't miss a beat if there was anything depending on his face card.

He matched the perfect image of a new and developed protégé. One who mastered the steps without having to repeat the cycle. He was bound to lead the entire family on his back and he proved that with every gloomy day that crawled by. Instead of inviting Janita's attitude. Rika thanked her and headed for the guest room until Halo decided what was next.

The tension could be felt, but Sonya refused to allow it to get any breathing room. The comment wouldn't stop escaping her lips until everyone understood. Kimmi was a target with each day that passed, and the emotional sessions would have to remain tucked until Kimmi was back in the comfort of their arms.

"It's settled, Sonya, tomorrow we're sliding inside the Louie hangouts and catching us a few down bad until we find something. However, many we have to eliminate or flip in order to get the little one back home. Everyone else can place the time into finding extra places for us to have on standby. This will start loosening the mix up for sure. Rex is supposed to meet Tipton tomorrow with his weekly payment and I'm going to rise up and fill God's spot being that he isn't here. Demon already has instructions on his position to assist us. So, it places the group in a position to focus. You all just need to be prepared," Halo said before his phone vibrated repeatedly.

He glanced at the screen, then picked up the long-distance number and listened for instructions, as she stepped out of the kitchen. Halo moved through the living room, and headed out on the front deck, pressing the number five. The call was accepted and allowed them to begin speaking.

"Halo?"

"Yeah, God, I'm here." He waited quietly for his friend's instructions.

"Listen, bro, throw this line away when you hang up from this conversation. I need you to keep shit flowing with Rika. Tell her we need access and that's our way. The problem with Kimmi needs to be handled, I mean like yesterday. Even if we have to place two contracts on his head. I need you to get, my baby, Halo.

"I'm not gonna rest until she's in the safety of my arms, God. We putting it together to make sure, if it happens to go wrong, another plan will still be in effect."

"That's good, bro. I just need you to stay cool for me, Halo. I know how you might be feeling, right now, so keep tunnel vision. He's going to get in touch with you, the rest can unfold from there. No slacking, no fumbling, it's nobody left but you guys bro. Make it flow and bring Kimmi home. I need to know you got my back on that?" Tipton wanted Halo to verify the duty of getting Kimmi back and of course, eradicating the minor issue with Rex. It was fun while it lasted, but Tipton had to teach his backstabbing ass the first rule of betrayal.

"It's going to be handled. I got your back, God! We can only piece it together and watch for the bait to be bitten. Once we lock-in, it'll be beyond everyone, God. Real talk," Halo made his decision while Tipton was aware instead of it being brought up later on down the line. Every time he spoke, the anger would flow through his voice.

Halo wasn't the average guy to endure pressure. If shit got tight. His actions would let loose before his brain could examine what was at hand.

"Halo, you're not relaxed, I can hear it through your tone. I know it's hitting heavy, right now, but you're the only hope with holding things together. I don't have nobody else, bro. So, I don't need you to crash. Don't move and finish before we get to start. It's gonna play out, Halo. You gots to trust me on this," Tipton begged for his cooperation.

"You know it's whatever you say, God."

"Thanks, bro. Tell Janita I'll be calling in the morning, once I'm booked in. I'll find a better way to communicate. We need a fresh line."

"I'm waiting for the call, God. We not gon' move hastily, but I'm not allowing shit to go sour. It's my duty," Halo agreed.

"Tomorrow watch for my call. He's supposed to meet around ten a.m. so make it seem as if all is normal. I have to go, bro. Please take care of my family." Tipton exhaled into the receiver.

"Just prepare to come home, God. We standing full firm out here. No outsiders, all is still well and moving."

"Say less, bro, I'm out."

"Later, God," Halo huffed lightly and prepared himself for the position that was upon him now. The thought of all the girls only forced more borders around his mind to keep all affairs discreet. Halo knew that Tipton would be willing to lay down and die if the shoe was on his foot. So, it forced him to protect and serve every last woman Tipton cared for. That was the true power that bonded them closer than Brothers.

"Forgive me," Halo mumbled looking up into the pitch-black sky.

Heading back inside, he filled everyone in on Tipton's request. It didn't take much to understand his orders and Halo was sure to record them all into his memory and enforce the necessary buttons to make it all fall through.

"Tomorrow marks the start. Play y'all position and watch how it forms together."

Demon, Janita, and Sonya listened with close ears as Halo explained thoroughly. After touching on every base, he knew nothing more was needed to be said. The crew was in effect, but this time felt different. He could smell victory. There were no chances involved. It was either rock hard or get pimped out of the game for a memory. Nodding in silence, Halo tossed his emotions away and decided to wait patiently for Rex's phone call. The main mission was simple, get the baby girl of their family back.

Chapter 6
11:58 p.m.

Atlanta Federal Holding Facility

The loud buzzing door sounded off loudly allowing Tipton to enter the medium size dayroom. The stench of Pine-Sol and musty showers lingered freely through the air. It housed no more than thirty men, you could see a head peeking through the small windows that was centered towards the top of every cell door.

"White, you're in cell 28!" the guard who escorted him spoke with a loud voice that wasn't required unless you attended boot camp.

Tipton stood in front of the cell and waited as the slow medal contraption opened to let him enter the six by ten cell. The toilet was sitting on the right-hand wall and a small desk was packed in a small corner. It was opposite from where the bunks rested and a thin window flap sat on the wall directly across from him. The room resembled a motel 8 minus the stove. The bottom bunk was empty, and Tipton wasted no time placing his bed on the cold steel. The loud shuffling movements forced his roommate to roll over before the officer closed the cell door behind him. His bunkmate's skin was bright tan with a head full of silky hair. The thick mustache assured Tipton that he was clearly Mexican and it wasn't for sure if he got along with niggas or not. Tipton placed his back against the wall, nodded, and greeted him out of respect.

"What's good, my friend? The name's, Tipton."

The man leaped off the top bunk standing 5.8 at the most. A few Cuban chains hung lightly around his neck, and the stern look he wore was surely not an act. "The name's, Churro," his thick accent echoed through the room. Churro shook his hand, and pulled a rolled cigarette from the side of his bunk, then pulled a lighter from his joggers. He sparked it and held it towards Tipton.

"No, thank you."

Churro shrugged off his decline and took a seat at the small desk. "So, where you from Tipton?"

"From Atlanta."

"Atlanta, this place is flooded with all types of hustles Tipton. What did you have your hands in to land you in the Feds house?" Churro pulled on the nicotine with a straight face.

"A little sale charge, nothing that should have me here too long." Tipton took a seat on the edge of his bunk.

"*Sales charge*? You have to mingle with Kilos in order to touch this building, baby. A little sale charge doesn't exist in the bounds of this court and law."

"Tipton smirked but refused to answer the question."

Churro chuckled and held up his hand. "You don't really have to answer that. I'm kind of good with judging someone on first appearance. I know you might not want to express what you're locked up for, but that's good. Make it a routine until you know who the fuck you're dealing with," Churro warned before taking another drag of his nicotine.

Tipton folded his arms while glancing around the small cell. "You ain't gotta worry about me being in your way, bro. I stay to myself and I respect the prison flow no matter how it flows."

"It's not me you have to worry about. You'll understand once you get a feel for the dorm. Everyone respects me around here, so I'll never allow that to change regardless of who I'm sharing this hellhole with. If you're hungry, feel free to grab something out of the box, besides that. Welcome to the Breezy." Churro said to Tipton before climbing back into his bed.

A few things he spoke on crossed Tipton's mind once he stepped inside of the facility. Trouble was easy to find but damn sure hard to get away with if you happened to take a motherfucker's life behind the institution walls. You would be immediately transferred to maximum security. More than likely, you would accept your life sentence after a few days of being locked away. The Federal penitentiary was a different league. It was easy to get shit twisted, and placed in the mix of a sticky predicament, which is the reason Tipton focused on listening, instead of speaking. If things happened as planned, the process would be over quickly, and the jail cell would only be another memory.

Tipton began to place his plastic mat and covers together, then glanced up at his bunkmate. "Ay, Churro?"

"I'm listening," he replied still facing the wall.

"What the hell is the Breezy?"

"Our dormitory, the rules are easy, and the movement is established. If you turn out to be an imposter or the word about anyone pulling foul business gets stabbed immediately. It's rough my friend, but some days are better than most. If a person causes a problem, he'll be gone before you can blink twice. Like the wind," Churro explained.

The room grew silent, that gut feeling told Tipton to expect the bullshit if the hardheads of the dorm took his silence for weakness. Going home was a firm check that he couldn't detour away from, but he wasn't hesitating on beating a few niggas ass to make sure the disrespect ended wherever it started. Tipton laid down on his bed after storing away the small bag of property. The thought of his last bid haunted his vision with Dejavu. He pictured himself sitting back in prison once before and he was now reliving that moment once again. All the mistakes of befriending the wrong people. The lack of his mind when shit started to flip completely against what he already placed into effect.

Tipton rolled over to face the wall and exhaled deeply. He knew prison wasn't sweet. It was all part of maintaining and standing firm. The rest would unfold once Tipton resolved all his personal issues. He closed his eyelids, trying to get some rest before the morning found its way around. A small image of Rex dropped right on his mind. His skin was brown as clay and the dark smile he formed forced his cheekbones to slightly split open. Quickly opening his eyes to shake the thought, Tipton shuffled, until he ended up on his back.

It was so hard to take it all in. The fact of being consumed in a place were men promoted violence harder than their children's religion or productive activities. It was the slums for a reason, Tipton just hoped it didn't remove his new process of thinking. The brighter day was painted vividly, and if he conquered his problem without crashing. The last laugh was surely gonna be his instead of the ones who formed against him. Finding a comfortable position, Tipton's eyes slowly closed, allowing him to fall into a deep sleep.

Chapter 7
9:51 a.m.

After waking from his sleep to the sound of Tipton's phone buzzing repeatedly. Halo picked it up and quickly answered. "Hello?"

"I sent the address to your inbox. It takes fifteen minutes to arrive here from your crib," Rex taunted before hanging up.

Halo sat for a second and decided to accept the meetup. Rex was moving so quick he didn't notice Halo's voice speaking, instead of Tipton. It showed his impatience, and that's exactly where the group preferred him to be. The time for business was about to be presented and all negotiations were about to be addressed. Being sure not to raise Rex's bitch radar. Halo made sure he came alone to discuss whatever request, or agreement necessary for Kimmi to be handed over. Retrieving his car keys and gun from the living room table, he left quietly out of the house.

Halo arrived at the destination within twenty minutes. The half-empty plaza he turned inside didn't seem to alert any suspicion. After driving past a few parked cars, Halo's eyes roamed the area until he spotted Rex leaning against the hood of his Lexus. Halo slowed the truck down, pulled in front of him and turned the engine off. When he stepped out of the driver's seat, Rex's face frowned with disappointment. Being sure to watch his every mood. Halo slightly closed the distance leaving a few feet between them.

Rex clutched his pistol letting Halo know that he was close enough. "Why in the fuck are you here? Where the slave master at?"

Halo glared into his eyes sensing the fear. He fidgeted with the handle of his gun as if he didn't know whether to make a move. There was no sight of Kimmi and Halo didn't need a bad encounter while the whereabouts of Tipton's child remained unknown.

"I'm here on God's behalf. He's handling a little run-in with the law and needed me to be here to ensure things go accordingly."

Rex smirked with pleasure. "Oh, really? Now, what the hell happened to all that good dicklip popping about being so strategic? So, I'm assuming he's locked up if he couldn't be here right now on behalf of Kimmi, right?" Halo held eye contact and shrugged without a response. The feeling of victory moved through Rex when he glanced down to the bag in Halo's hand. "Is that my money?" "Could be. Where is, Kimmi?" Halo questioned.

"Kimmi is fine but that's not your concern. The deal was two hundred and fifty grand a week or five million upfront. Once that cash is paid in full she'll be returned unharmed," Rex specified with authority.

"If I give you the entire five. How can I guarantee you'll cover your end with bringing her back? You could just easily run and never fulfill your obligations. How do we even know if she's still alive?"

"Because Captain Angel, there's a purpose for everything in life, and she's only gonna die unless you idiots make the wrong action. Kimmi is safe and I don't need to keep the baby after the deal is complete. You can have her back, I'm holding her for one purpose. To ensure that y'all get my fucking drift on what I asked for. If you bring me five, I'll set a location for you to drop the money off. After I check the number. You'll get a second call on where to pick the brat up," Rex stated. "Now from the looks of it, you don't have the entire amount. So, toss that bag and let's began this process."

Halo could feel his anger rising as Rex babbled away. He didn't want to go against Tipton's word by killing him, but the role Rex was currently playing left him with a bad itch. He was trying to extort for cash and have his safety ensured by keeping the child hidden. It was obvious, whether he handled the business correctly or not, there was a possibility Tipton would have him murdered any day now. That was one thing Halo knew his scary ass feared. Tossing the bag over to Rex's feet, Halo cracked his knuckles in frustration.

"Look, Rex, Kimmi is a baby. An innocent child that has nothing to do with you and God's past. He's willing to give you the money and let this incident fly under the rug if you give her back to me. He doesn't want to differ with you."

Rex opened the bag in front of him and zipped it back after examining the money. He cleared his throat, sparked a blunt and gave Halo a nonchalant grin. "If you listen, shit will go correct. I'm not dumb by a long shot and I still have my own ass to watch out for. Remember, I could easily give her back today, but that wouldn't add up to my reason for doing this in the first place. Once he obliges with paying weekly. I'll think of a swap date to pay the rest. Until then, y'all need to make sure my money is being made. I'll be in contact, Magic Mike." Rex smirked before climbing in his Lexus.

Halo watched him pull smoothly out of the parking lot, there was nothing he could do about. In order to get shit handled, he would have to place his muscle down, but more quietly than usual. All it took was the right info on his location and everything inside besides Kimmi would be eliminated. Halo picked up his phone and dialed Sonya's number.

She answered on the second ring. "Yes?"

"Are you still in place?" he responded before getting back in the car.

"Yes, it's still the same. Two men and no sign of the other guy," Sonya confirmed.

"That's because he just left from in front of me. Keep watching, if you see him show up. Alert me and make your way back."

"I gotcha, Love. I'm staying on duty until we get some results," she assured before hanging up.

Halo slid the cell in his pocket and pulled out of the shopping plaza. The fate of everything Tipton loved and owned was at stake. Demon was the only key that could possibly help Halo change that. The business side didn't intrigue him and establishing the drugs for the clientele was the last thing on his list. His mind wouldn't rest until his friend's little Queen returned.

***

The sound of a knock erupted on the front door, causing Janita to quickly hop out off the couch. Halo left without anyone being aware, and she prayed that he was returning with a better update. Peaches opened the door, mumbled under her breath, and pushed passed her as if she was just the household cleaner.

Janita's patience was thin when it came to disrespect. So, she didn't hesitate on checking her bullshit. "Excuse me, but I didn't invite you in, Peaches."

Ignoring Janita's remark, she sat down on the couch. "You've never invited me in. My child's father did, this is his shit. Remember?" Peaches gave her a dirty look before pulling out her cellphone.

"I wouldn't care, this is my house also, and I'm not tolerating disrespect from anyone. Watch your mouth, because I don't have to allow you in my home. I accepted Tipton wanting all his close family and friends in one spot. That was only for the safety issue, sweetie. Don't push your luck."

Demon and Rika remained quiet, the energy level and mood were just beginning to simmer. Their minds were plotting for a smart move and it quickly disintegrated once the two women came in contact. The weird vibe with Rika was already enough for Janita. She didn't speak much, but when she did, it was only about Tipton, or Sleepy. That alone raised a red flag on her weird-ass. Now Peaches was making her way into the center for some damn attention and that shit was about to be squashed immediately. The nerve to destroy her dream art gallery and crash the wedding.

Peaches played one of the biggest parts for being a poor ass mama who was obviously hiding some extra shit. After four days of Kimmi being snatched, she still hadn't tried to contact the police about the matter. A real mother would never allow anyone to make a decision when it came to her children. It was beyond everyone's knowledge, but Janita had a great skill with reading people, and Peaches rated number one for the sneaky shit.

Peaches rolled her eyes at Janita and laughed. "It seems like someone is mad. Does it bother you, that my baby daddy really still loves me and is willing to do whatever to make sure I'm good?"

The remark caught Janita off guard, but it didn't stop her from clawing back. "Bitch you're a bum. He feels sorry for you and we still have bigger things like Kimmi to worry about. Matter fact, it's kinda crazy." Janita twirled her head in a funny motion. "I haven't seen you worry at all since we've been in this situation. You've left, and came numerous of times, and still have yet to secure the whereabouts of your baby. Now that's very weird. Does she even matter to you or is this only about my husband?"

"Bitch you bumped your head." Peaches stood up with her fists balled. "I'm the real one in case you didn't know, Janita. My daughter means the world to me something you might not know about. You still have support from your parents, Ms. Suburbs! I maintain because I know my child's father isn't dumb. He's a beast with the way he moves. I've watched him since he was a young teen. Tipton is gonna get our baby back, my faith is in that one hundred percent. You seem to be stressing harder than me. Do you think he's gonna fail? Are you really down like you say?" Peaches ranted to the point where Janita couldn't get a word out.

Rika stepped in between them right before Janita moved her arm to swing. "Maybe you two need to split away from each other for a second. I don't think Tipton would like this." She glanced back and forth between them.

"I think I'm getting hot in this bitch, anyway. I'll be on the back porch smoking my soul away if my child's father happens to call. I think it's time for us to have a real family talk," Peaches informed them before departing from the living room.

Janita watched her with a cold scold. The empathy for her child was real for the sake of Tipton, but there was no way Peaches could fix the chemistry between them. Her snake ways came from natural hate. That bitch couldn't touch her with a nine-foot pole and deep down, she wished for Janita's position. Her pride just wouldn't admit it. Tipton was gonna be supported enough by her, but if she was placing her wifey duties on the table. Peaches would have to be dismissed from their home until the smoke cleared.

"Ms. White, maybe this would be the time to explain what I meant by the phrase we spoke on yesterday?" Demon suggested.

"What are you talking about?" Janita took a deep breath to relax and listen.

Demon opened his brown, French, leather briefcase, and removed a monopoly board game. Rika watched as he held it up. He walked over to Janita and placed it in her hands, but her mind said to toss that shit across the room, especially when it didn't have shit to do with Tipton. She gave her second thought a chance to kick in, and still remembered that her husband placed these people around her for a reason. That shit held weight on her heart because it was never good to go against the grain of the one you sleep with.

"What am I supposed to do with this?" She gave him an irritated look.

Demon grinned. "Learn." He grabbed the box from her hand, opened it, and dumped the contents on their glass table, spreading the board open. He studied it for a second before placing his finger at the start line. "This is where Tipton's problem began. His friend is competing to win a race that no one is aware of. If you follow the trail, you will notice the available properties, and things available for sale. His friend chose not to buy and follow instead. That was until they reached a blockage, which is the next slot on the board, the *Go-To Jail* box," Demon said with emphasis to see if she was catching on.

Rika sat on the sideline listening for the first few seconds and eventually moved closer to the table with them. She remained quiet as Demon continued to speak.

"After the jail card is in effect, the one who remains on board begins to take control. He starts to buy property and place his hand in everything that seems worthy enough to build his name. He could easily stumble if he picks the wrong choice, but he would be in the lead. Not so much for the man who sits in jail and has it all taken away. When he is finally let out of the jail box. His come up will have to begin all the way at start. Tipton is that piece sitting behind that wall, right now," he explained with a straight face.

Janita could hear him clearly, but the explanation was scrambling her brain like burning eggs on a Sunday morning. "I don't know if you're being extra precise, or if I'm just having a hard time learning."

"He's using the board to give him direction." Rika gasped when she finally caught on.

"Who?"

"Rex," Rika confirmed grabbing two medal pieces, placing them on the start line. "If this was Tipton and Rex, it would have to be someone who's winning. Rex played the low-key role and saved his funds while letting Tipton bypass him with all the amazing work ethics. He placed things in order and once it came down to the end. Someone had to be placed in a cell, which is Tipton. Now, this would be the time for Rex to accumulate and build while proceeding. His competition will have to work in order to get out which makes the race slightly easier. Rex nearly grabs everything into a chokehold while the time bypasses, Tipton. Once he's released the money, and name will not be as strong which means he will be back at start. If you make it to the end of the board with everything and your opponent has nothing. You monopolized the entire game. Right now, place that in your mind, along with the Louie Gang lingo, *Live life like a game of monopoly.*"

"Rex is using a board game to outsmart, Tipton," Rika explained while dragging a finger from the start line to the end mark.

"Indeed," Demon approved with a positive nod.

Janita's mind was totally fucking twisted after piecing their theory together. What made things worse is the shit really made sense. Rex was building an organization around Tipton and using the opposite choices to create a ditch for him when it became too big. In the end, he wasn't going to allow anything to be in Tipton's possession. It finally made sense about him snatching Kimmi. The police raid and killing Tipton's main supporters Dejuan and Chocolate. He masterminded a way to trick him without breaking a sweat.

"I can't believe this, he's really playing by the rules of a fucking child's board game. What does that mean now? I've never seen anyone play by the rules at this game. So, I'm guessing that's what it means for us?" Janita doubted with uncertainty in her tone.

"No, it means you have to outthink him. It takes the right steps and actions," Rika mumbled while looking down at the board curiously.

Demon placed another medal piece on the square and slid it slowly pass each square. He continued all the way around until he reached the end. "You have to be the piece that slides through the obstacles without falling. It'll be harder because it has to be done strategically. If you move like him, his instincts will catch what you're doing and that's when you'll lose. We have to beat him by reversing things. Try obliging with his actions and show no emotions. It'll keep him lost and wanting to know why the reward was now being placed into his lap without using any effort. That's when he will expose his hand and you will know how to react. His posture was definitely backing up the conclusion. Rika was agreeing, judging from the way she nodded in silence.

Janita rubbed her face with two hands, before pacing in a circle. "I know what we need to do," she revealed before running the idea back through her mind thoroughly.

"What is it, will it make this nightmare come to an end?" Rika speculated on what Janita placed together.

"I'll need a minute to explain things better, but I know it's gonna take all of us to work together."

Rika folded her arms and took a seat. "For some reason, I believe you. I'm in, so this would be the time to break us in on what's next."

"We might need some extra things, but the main part is simple," Janita mentioned before locking eyes with Rika. "Seduction."

Chapter 8

The music booming through Rex's duck off spot was rattling the walls with aggression. As he stared at the bundles of cash resting on the kitchen counter, he popped another bottle of Patron and sat down with his three young protégés. The crew was small, but they all knew how to listen and comply. Jay, Mula, and Spud were hustlers by heart and all of them shared the same passion, getting bread and sliming whatever they could to eat. Instead of turning them down like the other businessmen. He embraced them to teach the important shit and showed action when it was time to confirm what he expected. After months of molding his young hotheads. They were finally graduating to do bigger shit.

"I just wanna thank y'all lil' nigga's for being true to the Louie. I know how it feels to not have shit and watch another motherfucker live life like a king. It's a hate that I developed when I was young, but I hide that shit well. I made a promise to myself that if I saw something you possessed that I'm in need of, I'll bargain until I get it. Even if that means me crossing you out to make it happen. It only happens to the clowns who deserve it." Rex smirked while filling all three of them a fresh cup. He grabbed the remote and lowered the music volume. His hands fumbled with a rolled joint and he couldn't help but to grin. "You three have shown me that tricking clowns is your specialty. That's what the Louie Gang is all about. If you make us lose, you lose."

"Like the Mario game, right? People stay losing that shit," Spud joked.

Rex chuckled with a nod. "Facts, like the Mario game. Yo' ass only gets so many tries before you can't come back, it's automatic. The game is set that way. Now is the time for niggas to know that y'all ain't just been selling weed for the past few months, but really learning some shit that can box in this entire city. We all can win." Rex threw the proposition on the table, stood up, moved towards the counter and tossed a few bundles of money into all three of their laps.

"What's this for?" Jay thumbed through the ten-grand of hundred-dollar bills.

"I was about to ask the same shit. Is this our new pay rate?" Mula chimed in.

Rex sparked his weed with a shrug. "You can make more if you want too. That all depends on how dirty you can play for the team?"

"Shit, for this much money, I'll play filthy." Spud smiled with a wicked facial expression.

"Good, I want y'all to feel that way. The mission has leveled up and we need more avenues. Get these spots established, and network with whoever speaking about some cheese. If it's not the color of my trees, then how can I be pleased?" Rex laughed.

Of course, the money would always beat the weak-minded when it came to actions or bad deeds. It was easy for Rex to pollute the minds of three teenagers who didn't mind playing the pieces to his game. Tipton was the man when it came down to showing all that fake ass love, but he damn sure didn't have the heart to be a leader overall. His emotions would fumble and crash the ship. Rex knew that he was never blessed coming up, and the men who were misusing their rewards for selfish reasons were common. It was time to show the youth how to control the streets. A way where no one could decode your steps unless they've played under you.

"What the hell are we 'bout to do about the little girl though, Rex? She can't stay in this bitch alone," Mula clarified.

"Don't worry about the kid. Just continue to make the drive like normal, the rest will come along the way," Rex encouraged before passing him the marijuana.

"I'll be right back? I just want y'all to keep Louie first, emotions last and mercy in the middle. That's our mission," Rex advised before leaving out of the kitchen.

The four-bedroom home he paced through was just the beginning of his new business. He was investing time on mastering the tricks of life and Tipton was his motivation. Turning down a long hallway, Rex stopped at the first room and peeked his head inside. Kimmi was stretched out on the bed sleeping peacefully. A Disney movie played on the flatscreen television that was mounted on the wall in front of her. Easing inside, he grabbed the remote and powered off the television. He glanced down at her resting face with a smile.

Rex shook his head. "In due time neicey pooh, it will all be handled," he whispered softly, then turned to leave.

***

Atlanta's Federal Holding Facility

12.45 a.m.

Tipton pulled the cover from his head after hearing the cell door open. He climbed out of the bed, quickly glanced out of the room and noticed all the bottom range doors slanging open.

"Rotation, rotation, fellas! Grab your shit, or stay inside," one of the Floor Officers crooned through the loudspeaker.

Noticing that Churro wasn't in his bed. Tipton shrugged and quickly grabbed the things he needed to wash. As he stepped out of the room, Tipton pulled the door up and moved toward the shower line. Noticing three sets of clothes hugging the rail. He knew the wait was just beginning. The dormitory was occupied with four showers and thirty plus men. Two different flatscreens occupied the floor area and most longterm inmates possessed a small handheld television inside their rooms. The vibe was thick and the only sound inside the Breezy was from selected channels on the trick box.

Men moved about sliding back and forth into other rooms. While most hung out on the top range with a stale face. The feeling of prison alone forced a person's mind to suspect some weird shit. The federal institution was like the modern world inside a cold steel box. The miscellaneous things as in smoking, killing, and gambling occurred on the regular. You would even see an inmate strike and fuck one of the nasty ass lil' guards when the opportunity presented itself. It was truly another hell on earth. Things could go smooth for months and one misunderstanding would have the medical staff rushing a motherfucker out to the free world hospital.

As Tipton pondered on his freedom and pretended to watch the *Love & Hip Hop Reality Show*. He glanced to his side and noticed three men walking calmly towards him. Their faces didn't signal any danger and Tipton knew his background stood firm in case one of them questioned him about anything. Most men would have looked away, but that script wasn't written like that in Tipton's mind. He watched them with a blank expression until they stood a small distance from each other.

"Waddup, guys, is there a problem?" Tipton's facial expression and tone had sucker written all over it.

The breeze house had the hounds who were willing to slide up on whoever. If you were off balance just by an inch with the way you treaded. The next morning your ass was receiving a breakfast tray with a few visitors added along. Tipton damn sure wasn't about to meet that day. Out of the three men, a short stocky bald guy with a small head moved forward.

"What it do, young goon. Where you from?"

His hands were waving around like he was thinking of trying some slick shit, so Tipton tightened his posture. "I'm from Atlanta."

"Cool, you from the spot. That's a good start." The man grinned. "My name is Buddha and these are my aces Splatt and Uno. It's our business to move around this bitch and ensure we on point with everyone that walks in that door. Last night we decided to let you sleep on in, but we happened to get a little word from the other dorms this morning that you was supposedly the man out there on the block?"

Tipton stared at the men with a pathetic frown, before turning his attention back to the TV. "Nah, bro, I think they got the wrong guy. I'm just a normal dude and I damn sure ain't running no block. Thanks for asking though."

Buddha leaned closer after hearing Tipton's response. His demeanor became more aggressive and his eyebrows curved with anger. "Aye little boy, that wasn't a debate. The info is conclusive. Your name Tip, right?"

Instead of replying with words. Tipton caved a hard two-piece to Buddha's chin and followed up with a stomach shot. The two men watched their dorm bully crash to the floor harder than a frozen bottle of water. Tipton wasted no time placing his guard back up to attack. Niggas was spilling out of their rooms and his last two opponents began clutching at their waist when Tipton slowly pushed towards them.

"Handle that shit, Splatt!" a distant voice yelled with authority.

The two dumb rookies were definitely shook from the way Buddha got his ass cleaned up. His face was still making out with the concrete and the natural instinct to kill them both was already in motion. It had to be done. Just when Tipton decided to proceed with his attack. Splatt snatched a sharp, ice pick from underneath his state shirt. His arm swung recklessly allowing Tipton to dodge his attack swiftly. Leaping back, he prepared for the men to rush him. Instead, they backed him down slowly into the corner and Tipton realized that Uno was also holding a knife. The battle became uneven within seconds. The thought of taking a war wound to disarm one of them was all he could picture in his mind. He just needed to reach at the right moment.

Splatt and Uno mugged him evilly as they closed the distance to handle their business. The bell of God was obviously ringing loudly because Churro appeared out a top row cell with seven dangerous Mexicans moving behind him. The machete's they carried was sharp enough to cut a man's neck into pieces with one hit. Churro cleared the way as he walked and jumped directly in front of Tipton. He pointed his knife at Splatt forcefully and uttered something loudly in Spanish. Tipton surely didn't deny his assistance, and whatever Churro blurted out caused the Mexican men around him to get slightly belligerent. Their knives were ready to talk and Churro wouldn't hesitate to call the final word. His wide eyes searched for any sign of aggression, and it was well known about the incidents Churro participated in since he was incarcerated. That reason alone forced the two assholes to quickly back up.

"Listen, man, he's my bunkmate. So, ain't nobody jumping, or taking anything if it involves him, Comprende?" Churro raged.

His sharp meat cleaver shook violently with every word that spilled from his lips. That shit instantly got the dormitory quiet as the pastor's church on Bible study night.

Tipton stood behind the group of Mexicans to calm his adrenaline before stepping forward. "Churro, I don't want to be a problem for you. You can stand down, I'll—"

Churro ignored his request before he could even get the sentence out of his mouth. "No, that's not how it goes with me, Tipton. If they have a problem with you, they can deal with me also," he stressed with his jaws clenched tightly.

Splatt didn't want to feel like a pussy in front of his blood gang homies, so denying Churro's call for war had to be straightened immediately. A few more inmates protruded from the rooms with towels around their necks, knives were being clutched by at least forty five percent of the dorm, and Tipton didn't know who was riding for who. The tension was heavy. Churro's small army was moving around shirtless, and tattoos covered most of the Mexican's faces and stomachs. Even though they were outnumbered. The heart and fire inside them forced the majority to bow down and talk.

Splatt held his hands up out of respect before addressing Churro. "This is between us, my friend. I don't mean any disrespect, but this is something personal from the street. He can shoot the fade with me. If he loses his ass gotta pack it up."

Uno butted in quickly, "Let him fight like a man. He ain't talking about shit without y'all help. Yall protecting niggas now?" he fumed gripping his weapon tightly.

"Fuck you, punto! We will eat you motherfuckers if that's what you want, man!" Churro snapped stepping forward.

Tipton grabbed his arm before he could pop off. His eyes pleaded with understanding. "Churro, I'll fight him, it's okay. I don't want it to go viral about this bullshit if he's asking to see me man to man. If anything opposite happens, I'll be grateful for your assistance, but I gotta handle this."

Churro glared into his eyes with major respect for the courageous heart. Knowing the pride of a man was number one, he nodded and stepped to the side. Churro pointed at Splatt and agreed with a final statement, "If you attempt to touch him with a blade. I will kill every last motherfucker standing within a ten-foot radius from you."

The dorm formed a large circle which was the original way to shoot a fair fight. The Mexicans and Churro moved behind Tipton as he entered the circle without debating. Splatt slowly made his way to the center. His posture spelled nervousness, but Tipton still wouldn't underestimate him. It took a while for the dorm to start the sixty-second clock.

Once the time started, all the blood members began to chant. "Yoooo! Whooooppp!"

The phrases musta truly meant a lot to Splatt, because once his ears got a small sound of that. He grew comfortable and threw up his guard.

Tipton nodded with respect before throwing up his hands. They circled each other for a few seconds. The dorm's noise was starting to rise and it placed the battery pack inside of Splatt's back to swing.

Tipton used his sidestep and landed a hard kick to his side. Splatt stumbled but didn't go down. The loud grunt he released allowed his weakness to be revealed. His bitch ass couldn't take to many more of those. After testing the water for a few seconds. Tipton stepped inside his personal space and landed four solid blows. Splatt stumbled but replied with a hard, left hook.

Feeling the hard punch land perfectly. Tipton shook it off and reminded himself to dodge the next one quicker. The blows were exchanged equally, but Tipton was much faster. After forty seconds into the fight, Splatt began to grow tired and slow. He held his ground swelling Tipton's bottom lip severely, but the sweat was pouring profusely down his forehead, forcing him to swing a haymaker. Splatt visioned himself missing and that was the last thing he remembered before Tipton's vicious uppercut put him to sleep.

The sound of Splatt's bone cracking caused everyone to flinch in shock. His body deflated to the ground, Tipton didn't hesitate to stand over him and release his second wind.

"Wake up bitch!" he snapped while punching him repeatedly.

Splatt's face split with every blow that landed and the clock was signaling the end, forcing Churro to snatch Tipton off his ass before the fight turned into a murder.

Pulling him back, he lightly tapped Tipton's cheek to break his anger state. The entire dorm stood around quietly, while the Mexicans formed their circle back around Tipton. Churro proceeded to the center floor and watched as Buddha helped Splatt to his feet. His head was swollen with numerous of knots.

Buddha put a shirt over his friend's bloody face, before Churro spoke, "Do we still have any problems, my friend?" his voice boomed with victory.

Buddha shook his head. "It's over, Churro, the little nigga won man. It's nothing else to prove," he stammered with his excuse.

Tipton stood shirtless with his muscles flexing from the slight workout. After Churro ended the conversation with Buddha. He moved with his men to walk Tipton to their cell. The large crowd eventually began to disperse, and Churro's horrible mug flipped upside down when they entered the room.

"Tipton, you're a very good fighter. I didn't expect that out of you," he boosted the hype of his win. The news was probably halfway around the institution, and nothing was kept a secret in the Breezy. "I respect you, Tipton. You have heart, and honor. It makes me feel good to call you a friend. Whenever there's a problem my men will assist you. I'll make sure we're always good in here. If you connect with me and be a part of my team while you're away from home. It's nothing better than learning the language for your trips, Tipton." Churro smiled with anticipation.

Nodding, Tipton cursed himself for getting back involved with shit that led him to prison. Behind the walls could lead to more than just an injury. You could possibly die and never make it out. Until the time presented itself. Tipton guessed that a little learning classes with Churro wouldn't be too bad. He wiped the blood from his lip and looked up at him. "I'm pretty good at cooking. You know anything about burritos?"

Churro smiled from ear-to-ear, before whistling for one of his assistants.

Chapter 9

The day was moving by slowly like the end was near. The hot sun from earlier was gone, but still had the air humid, and thick. Night-fall was about to conquer the sky and Janita was finally getting a small piece of mind after Peaches took it upon herself to leave. All she did was forge more pain and irritation on everyone because of her own slick ass guilt. Her slime ass ways weren't blinding nobody, but Tipton. Not only was Peaches to old for him when they met, but her child that she conceived by him was definitely not her first priority. She pushed around forcing people to be sad by telling lies and scamming. Anything to get more money out of someone because Tipton damn sure wasn't giving her a dime for sure.

Hearing the sound of a soft engine pulling inside of their drive-way, Janita raised up from the hood of her car and eyed the mysteri-ous Black Sedan parking smoothly at the center of their entrance. The lights cut off and the engine settled. Janita didn't waste any time getting her ass up in case she had to make a run for it. Whoever was in the damn car obviously didn't belong if Halo wasn't aware of anyone just randomly showing up to Tipton's home.

Just when Janita was about to go alert Demon. The driver's side door opened and Sincere stepped out. "Nita," he whispered loud enough to get her attention.

She paused in her tracks, turned and spotted her dumb ass broth-er creeping up the driveway like a cat burglar. Being sure that no one was coming out of the house, she moved towards him cautious-ly. Her angry facial expression said enough.

Sincere honestly didn't know what to say to begin their conver-sation, "Look, Nita—"

"What the hell are you doing here, Sincere? Tipton wants to kill you. How in the hell could you tell me about the grimey shit you did to my husband and come here like he ain't out looking for you?" she fumed with a low stern tone.

Sincere glanced behind her again to be sure they were alone. "Nita, I never told on him. They're only using me to trick him. I never told them anything, I lied," he stated truthfully.

Janita held up her hand in a dismissive manner. "It's nothing that you can tell me. I don't even know what to say about you, Sincere. Halo is gonna be back here any minute now. I don't think Tipton needs to hear about you being spotted here."

"Janita you don't understand. You're in danger if you stay here. This is something beyond your control. These people are out for Tipton and they're gonna take you down with him, forever Nita. His cases are so backed up that they could throw out two of them right now and still have enough to give him two life sentences. Rex is going to tear everything Tipton built to pieces. He's been a fucking snitch the entire time. I don't think you see what's about to happen and I'm trying to warn you," Sincere pleaded with a desperate frown.

Janita knew her brother was family, but his disloyalty severed their personal relationship to pieces. Tipton was her husband and the fact of going against him period forced her to feel that his current situation was caused because of Sincere. Trusting anybody was just a chance she couldn't take at the time.

"You need to leave. Tipton needs me, Sincere. I don't care about who's lying or not. It's not gonna bring him home, I'll be fine. You just worry about yourself." She turned to walk away from him.

Sincere grabbed Janita's arm and closed his eyes for no longer than five seconds. "Sis, Rex is going to kill you if this doesn't end, right now—tonight. You don't know what he's capable of doing, Janita. He's been planning this shit since the beginning. You have to come with me." Sincere pulled her arm slightly towards him.

Janita snatched back and gritted on her teeth. "Just leave, Sincere. I'm not leaving, I'm never leaving. I can't just run and abandon, Tipton, for every little thing he goes through. You have to live your life just like I have to live mine, Sincere. Maybe you should stop wasting it, worrying about me," Janita explained calmly before glancing behind her. She didn't need Rika and Demon giving a third-degree investigation when she made it back inside from her alone time. They'd spoken about safety constantly for the past few days, so Sincere standing in front of her would have been the first breach. "Please leave, I don't want Halo or anyone else to go against Tipton's words or trust." Janita wanted to see him leave instead of dying. "You need to be out of my driveway in thirty seconds, or I'm gonna happen to forget exactly who you are the next time I peak out of my blinds."

Sincere couldn't believe her remark, but it cut hard enough to let him know shit wasn't a fairytale. He shrugged with a pathetic mug, turned on his heels and jogged slowly back over to his car.

Janita watched until he got inside the car and started the engine. By the time she reached the front door of her home, his car was gone with the wind. Janita exhaled knowing that her brother needed more than a few cops to fix his role in the matter. Tipton was coming home, regardless of what it took, but if you were against him, you were damn sure against her. Even if that meant watching her own brother suffer for his mistakes. Tipton was not only her motivation. He put life back in Janita. Happiness didn't flow for years of her life, but she managed to bounce back with Tipton that was all she needed and it was time to start showing exactly how hard she was willing to stand on that.

Chris Green

Chapter 10
11:26 p.m.

Eastside of Atlanta: Peaches' Mother's House

The tingly feeling in Peaches' body started to spread when she leaned down snorting the last line of molly. Her little secret fuck buddy, Kap was watching closely knowing she was about to do a repeat of the freaky shit she pulled thirty minutes earlier. Her nature for sex got explicit when she was tweaking off the drugs. Besides dealing with her nasty ass attitude, Kap enjoyed fucking whenever they got a chance for some free time and that was enough for him. Peaches leaned her head back from the nose run approaching.

"You need to slow down. We ain't gon' be able to snort anything, later on, I got a gram left." Kap fumbled with a small baggie between his fingers.

Peaches rolled her eyes. "Then you just gonna have to get some more. I paid my bills and my shit running low until next month," her tone was snappy.

"What the hell you yelling for? I'm just trying to prepare your ass cause I'm tapped out to shawty. I spent four hundred dollars on molly just in four days of us kicking it together, Peaches."

"Well, find somewhere else to chill then." Peaches waved him off.

Kap laughed and pushed her hand. "Just calm down, I'll get some more. You gotta stop getting so damn emotional. Have you a cigarette or something." He tossed a pack of Newports in her lap.

Peaches gave him a disgusted look before picking up her phone. She dialed the last number and waited patiently to see if he would answer. It didn't take long for the voicemail forwarding to dance through her ear. It was the seventeenth call made to him within two hours, and still, there was not one reply.

"Who the hell you keep trying to call Peaches? Obviously, them folks don't wanna talk." Kap stood off the couch to stretch his legs.

"Please can you shut the fuck up!" Her bipolar mug was flashing hard.

Kap knew she could get out of her body when it came down to disrespect. Still, he wasn't about to deal with the crazy tongue. "Peaches watch yo' mouth shawty. I been back and forth in yo' momma spot for the past four days with you. Buying food, drugs, whatever. I'll just leave if you keep acting like that shit don't mean nothing," he taunted with his hands in the air.

Her phone buzzing ceased the conversation before she could reply and give his young ass the business. She picked it up and rose from the couch heading for the kitchen. After making sure Kap couldn't ear hustle on her business spoke lightly. "Hello?"

"There has to be a valuable reason why you calling my fucking phone like a bombing just occurred in Magic city's strip club, cause that's the only way I'm taking my attention off what I'm doing, right now," Rex stated before she thought of saying some stupid shit.

"Nigga, you know what the fuck I'm calling for. It's been nearly five days. That was the max time limit we agreed on," Peaches whispered into the cellphone.

"I know what the fuck today is. But at the same time we never agreed on your man getting booked either, now, did we? I need my money, all of it. Just have patience," he assured her with a tone of domination.

"What? Rex, stop playing with me. You said she would be gone four to five days. The plan didn't work idiot, you can get your money in increments, and I'll keep her away until you've gotten the agreed cut that Tipton was gonna pay. I don't care, but I need my baby back today," Peaches ordered.

Rex laughed hard before getting extremely serious. "She ain't coming back until I say so bitch!"

His statement caused her heart to pace faster. "What! If you don't want me to get the police involved then you need to bring Kimmi to me, right now, Rex."

"And if you don't wanna find yo' punk ass baby stuffed inside a vacuum-sealed trash bag, you'll stop with all the police games hoe. Peaches, I don't know if you think I'm something to play with, but I can show ya that's a stupid way of thinking. I'll bring her to you, right now. Just give me the address?" The thought of him killing her stupid ass would make shit twice as easy. There wouldn't have to be no second-guessing or worrying about the ties of his business. Either she was gonna move accordingly or get found dead in the bathroom of her spot. It wasn't a such thing as debating.

Peaches took a deep breath knowing shit was about to go further than expected. "Don't you think this is a little overboard? You got a free lump sum of money and Tipton is locked up. Why can't you settle for that? All I want is my baby," she pleaded.

"And I said you're gonna get her back. Kimmi is fine, but I still have business conducting with them. Once I'm done, I'll fix it all back. You just gotta ride with my word on this. You agreed, remember?"

Kap appeared around the corner locking eyes with Peaches. His shirt was off and his handheld a rolled blunt. She raised a finger to make sure he didn't speak.

"Rex, get whatever you need and bring her back. I'll wait two more days. After that the deals off." Peaches hung up without giving him another option.

Kap moved over to her with a curious look. "You okay?"

"Yeah. Where the sack at?" She flipped his question around smoothly.

He dug inside his pocket and held it up in the air. "Nah, if I give you this shit. I don't want none of that snappy, depressed, Peaches. That shit be killing the mood shawty?"

"Boy ain't nobody worried about me being mad, but you. I'll be just fine." She took it from his possession. He stood in front of her smiling hard as hell.

Peaches grinned. "What the hell you staring for?"

"Because I wanna eat some pussy." He gripped his dick with aggression.

His print always did it. Sex with Kap ended with a lot of nasty ass talking and long stroking. He didn't lack when it came down to some action. His soft, ass caring side forced her attraction to show easily.

Peaches looked at his chiseled young muscles with a smile. "Why you trying to entice me, nigga? You know what you doing."

"I ain't never had to entice you before. You said the pussy cry for me, right?" He slowly pulled down his pants, letting his stiff monster hang.

Peaches kitty jumped with happiness and her mouth watered with anticipation to taste it again. She looked at him hungrily and grabbed his shit, stroking it lightly. It began to grow before her eyes. Heading down south, Peaches deep throated his shit, placing a long trail of spit down his shaft. Then she rubbed it around his wood with a freaky smile. She started sucking that dick with a vengeance. All his meat was gliding down her throat and she welcomed it with the nasty gag sounds he loved. Peaches rubbed her titties in satisfaction. Her pussy was in heat for some beating time and Kap was damn sho 'bout to handle it. He fucked her mouth the strong way, fast and slow. It was so sexy watching her mouth down all his package like a true professional.

"Shittt, Peaches!" he grunted from her moans and mouth rising louder.

He pulled his dick from between her lips, unbuttoned her jeans and slid them down to her ankles to take off. He gently kissed different sections of her body with affection until she kicked the pants from around her feet. He grabbed her hand, making her hike that round ass up in the large kitchen chair. Peaches had just enough space to bury her head low and ass high for great access. Her honeypot pulsated with every move she took. Kap was known to go deep and his young ass wouldn't hold back anything when it came to demonstrating that shit.

Examining her perfect arch mounted up on the huge wooden chair. He positioned himself behind her and grabbed Peaches' soft ass. He plunged his dick slowly into her wet cat.

"Ohhh, God!" Peaches legs fidgeted when he dropped that nine-piece balls deep. After making sure she adjusted to his length. He started his pound game like usual. Within two minutes Peaches' ass cheeks were spread wide while he slammed into her shit like it was his last night alive.

"Kappp! That shit in my guts, daddy! It's in there," she panted before busting a good orgasm over his manhood. He could see that sweet, sticky caking up around the rim of her pussy. The more he pumped, the faster it flowed.

"I can't breathe," Peaches whispered while holding the edges of her chair for dear life.

The wind from him sliding out of her to the tip of his dick caressed her love button and the loud noise from her wet kitty erupted every time he went inside.

"Damn, Peaches, I got you baby." He closed his eyes when he felt that nut coming close. The sound of her large ass colliding with him forced him to spill his shit deeply into her belly. "Fuckkk!" he grunted in satisfaction.

"Sss—Kap, please," she moaned in a low tone when he pulled out of her treasure.

Catching his breath, he rubbed her round butt. "Can we finish this in the room?" He exhaled deeply with a passionate aura rising from his skin.

Peaches slowly slid off the chair and touched her cat with two fingers. That bitch was hurting, but Kap's piece felt so good handling her the real man way. She couldn't deny him. Giving his ass a sexy tongue kiss. Her hand bumped his dick that started to slowly swell up again.

"You can do whatever you want, daddy, but you can't leave. If you gonna beat this pussy like that, stay here with me to make sure I'm straight. My mom is out of town and I'm here for the next few days by myself," she offered with a sexy smirk.

He grabbed a hand full of ass and kissed her. "Well get that ass in the air, right now. Get yo' ass in that room." He slammed an open palm down on her ass cheek.

"Ooouuhhh," she hissed in pleasure. "You betta do all that good shit, too." She grabbed his hands to head for the back room.

The thought of him being there put her life on safe mode for at least a few days. In order to get the baby back, Peaches had to respect the boundaries she crossed with Rex. One way, or another, that word would never hit the airwaves for anyone unless shit started to look ugly. If he made one attempt to harm, Kimmi. The decision would be off her hands. Kap was gonna be right there for sure and he was enough man alone to make it happen.

Chapter 11

The morning sunshine was brighter than usual, Janita was finally able to get away from the house without the guys trying to dissect every move she made. After Halo and Sonya returned to the crib last night. They discussed Rex for hours it was a drag session of doubt, and it became clear that he was truly Tipton's worst enemy. All the new secrets from their past were slowly revealed. The plots of Vel sending Rex on a mission of destruction. Tipton finding out about the old DNA papers of his true biological father. The story was a jumbled mystery of a broken home. Out of Rex and Tipton's entire friendship, it exploded with a tragedy claiming the lives of close family and friends. It showed that things were deeper than everyone expected. On the strength and love she shared for her husband, Janita vowed to become whatever necessary to hold shit down until he returned.

Pulling into the driveway of her parent's home, Janita parked her car and headed inside. The one-level home was beyond sufficient for the elderly couple. It was a nice feeling to know that her mother's needs were catered for personally by the hands of her father. It was a solid foundation of structure something they taught during Janita and Sincere's youth days. They also molded them about honor of the family. To never stand against each other in a matter. That statement had officially been thrown out of the window. This was the step to a new life.

Janita walked through the front door and entered the kitchen where her mother and father sat quietly enjoying breakfast.

"Hey, yall." She placed a kiss on both of their cheeks, before taking a seat.

"Hey, baby girl. You look beautiful." Janita's mom got up to fix her daughter a cup of coffee.

"Thank you, mama." She forced a smile.

Janita's aura was surely different today. The normal, lovely, classy wear was replaced with a bossy, bad girl look. Her blue, bleached Valentino jeans were doing more than gripping her backside. The brown Alexander Mcqueen shirt matched her Sacai leather boots and the curly hairstyle switched to a normal, but attractive ponytail.

"When did you start wearing makeup, Janita? What has my son in law done to you?" Mr. Stanton chuckled before sitting down his newspaper to observe his princess closer.

"I'm just trying something new daddy. I came to talk about Tipton's situation." Janita jumped to the point, there was no need to beat around the bushes with her parents. Out of everyone she had near her side. Their understanding nature was normal when they suffered from tons of mistakes themselves, including through the times of their youth.

"Is there something wrong, Janita." Her mom placed a cup of Maxwell in front of her.

The worry on her daughter's face was distasteful. Janita was never a talkative child growing up. Her style was solo and a conversation from her was very rare. These times were now different, but her mother could sense that old fear lingering in the air.

Janita looked back and forth between her parents and processed her thoughts before speaking. "I told you guys about Tipton's situation. It seems like he ran into a little roadblock and had to straighten a few things with the law."

Her father folded his arms with a stern face. "I heard about it. Your mother told me, but I didn't receive the full story. Is there any specific reason he's having this issue?"

"Yeah, your son," Janita informed before taking a swig of her coffee.

"Excuse me?" Mr. Stanton leaned forward after Sincere's involvement was mentioned. "What do you mean, my son?"

Janita's mom sat back confused also. It was the first time Sincere's name sounded so guilty coming from their daughter's mouth. Her tone was dry and disgusted. Things didn't usually get to Janita, so her mom could see that it was clearly a serious problem at hand.

Her father sat up straight, preparing to hear evidence of what transpired. "Baby girl, now I know your brother could be difficult sometimes. I'm not saying this just to make your mom upset. But what does your brother have anything to do with Tipton being arrested? Janita, he's a drug dealer baby girl. Nothing good comes from that. So, where does Sincere come in all this?" He put a hand on his chin.

He showed no form of empathy in his eyes or tone, and the bashing talk of his son was obviously not clear enough for his old ass to soak in.

Janita, repeated herself, "Sincere snitched on my damn husband, daddy. He got him arrested. Now I'm not dumb, so being aware of Tipton's dealings is nothing new to me. Sincere on the other hand knew about this and chose to deal with him. Through all this, crooked and illegal narcotics getting sold. He decided to work with the police to bring Tipton down instead of being a man."

"Janita, be mindful of your language, please. That's your father." Ms. Stanton stood up with a disappointed face. "Now I don't know what your brother has gotten into, but I haven't spoken to him in days. What would make him want to do that to your husband? Is there something he did to Sincere for this to happen?" She accused not wanting to believe the shocking news.

Mr. Stanton waved a hand to stop his wife. "Hold on dear, because I'm lost here. Why would my son have to tell on a man who's knee-deep in the game? That boy been dealing smack since you introduced us to him. The entire family heard this clearly at the wedding. What makes things so different now? Because Sincere wasn't around then." He questioned as if that dumb statement cleared his son from being a snitch.

Janita shook her head in disbelief. "Wow dad, you really feel that he wouldn't? I listened to him tweak out on the phone for hours that night. A guilty conscience will give it away. He told me about the interrogation with the detectives himself. The fire under his ass was beginning to burn and he couldn't handle it."

"Janita watch your mouth when you address me, young lady!" Her dad shoutedJanita continued to speak over his voice. "It burnt so hard that he took the fucking coward way and had my husband taken away from me! I'm not watching my mouth. I'm a grown-ass woman, and this isn't my damn boyfriend were speaking about. He's my husband!" Janita snapped, her leg rocked at a fast pace and the insult about Tipton began to rumble with her anger.

True colors about the way her dad felt were finally coming out. His mind felt that Sincere could do no wrong. A frequent emotion that he carried since their youth. The matter was far more serious than their childhood issues and Mr. Stanton refused to allow the fake ass real nigga image to be under the name of his only son.

"Janita Stanton, I love you, but I'm really close to asking you and your disrespectful energy to leave without coming back," he threatened, his eyes started to bulge with anger.

"Ronald and Janita Stanton!" her mama yelled over them until the arguing finally ceased. "What in the hell has gotten into you two?" Her mind was trying to gather all that was being said, truthfully she was beyond disgusted. "Family don't just quit like nothing can't change. We just come down to a resolution to make it better!" her mom's voice boomed.

Janita thought about her next move and didn't wait to hesitate. She stood up to her feet and pulled out a piece of paper with a small number on the front. Then she pushed it across the table. Janita grabbed her purse and locked eyes with her bitter father. "I'll say this and make my departure from your home since I will never be returning. When I moved away to my own bills, love life and children. That became my daily life and responsibility to maintain. I worked hard to find a man I could love and build my own empire with. That man is Tipton. From this day on, nothing, not even you two will stop me from elevating with him or to forget what's best for my life. Tipton has a first appearance hearing in the morning. The federal courthouse downtown around eight-thirty. Apparently, your son is supposedly going to be there as the state's witness to force Tipton into trial. If he shows up to make one statement. Whatever happens to him will be out of my control," Janita addressed, her face showed no emotion, and that shit was stamped in the book if it came down to even a slight chance of losing Tipton.

"Is that supposed to be a threat, Janita? You're willing to let something occur against your brother about this. That has to be a joke. I wouldn't care if he said anything or not. He's still your flesh and blood," her dad raged from the cold ass remark she shot.

"Obviously, my life doesn't mean shit. I've explained to you that my husband is possibly facing a life sentence because of this. Not to mention his own personal problems. He may not mean anything to you two, but he treats me with love that none of you will ever be able to show. The one who gives me respect and loyalty like you two so-called showed us. It was your mission for me to find a King who would uplift me. That time has finally come true, but this is the same man you want to go down on the behalf of my weak ass flesh and blood. You might as well call Sincere for dinner and kill him yourself." Janita shrugged with a calm face, before turning to leave.

Mr. Stanton stood to his feet and started to give her a piece of his mind. "Now I've tried to have patience with this foolishness, but this will not be tolerated. Your attitude is unacceptable, and my son will not be bashed by his own sister, as if he isn't family in this home. Do you hear me Janita?" His voice was loud and trailing behind her ear as she headed out for the front door. Janita drowned the sound of his annoying ass voice cleanout. The decision was made. The disrespect that was being pushed around was about to end. Even if that meant getting rid of his ass to see it flourish. There wasn't a damn thing about to stop Janita's happiness and loyalty. She was willing to do whatever necessary to keep those words solid, any-thing.

Chris Green

Chapter 12

Light rain was slowly drizzling down from the sky, the sunny forecast was a failure as always on the outskirts of the city. Detective Sandra Elliot sat in the parking lot of the Federal Parole building, finishing the last of her Camel cigarette. Her appointment with Agent Witherspoon was twenty minutes behind and the case for tomorrow needed all the evidence possible to drown Tipton forever. Because of all the money, she was receiving it didn't matter who went down. The cash talked a thousand miles and her next payday was approaching very quickly. She stepped out of the black, tinted Dodge charger. Detective Elliot proceeded toward the entrance.

The cloudy sky was darkening by the minute and the slight drizzles started to thicken. Covering her head, she continued through the large parking lot. The sound of a vehicle pulling behind her forced the Detective to turn around. The approaching Lexus Coupé came to a smooth stop and the driver's window rolled down. Rex blew a cloud of his weed smoke toward her and sat back in the car seat.

"Ms. Sandra, that ass getting fat girl." He grinned.

"What in the fuck are you doing here?" Her eyes widened with anger.

"Calm down, I'm not trying to intrude with your daily duties. I know who you're coming to see. I just wanna be sure that me and you have an understanding. No one else is supposed to be aware of our business. You only had two missions, arrest Tipton and force Sincere to tell on his ass. That's what I agreed to pay for."

"No shit, Sherlock. You still realize that I have a real job, right? I have to place things in order for anything to fall as planned, but you showing up to a Federal office building isn't going to work." She stood in the rain with a heated expression.

"It may not, but you wanna know what it will do. It'll show you and every other motherfucker that I'm serious about my business. You're making deals with other people and that wasn't apart of the agreement bitch."

"What in the hell are you talking about?"

"I'm talking about, Mr. Kenny Quick, bitch. From what Sincere tells me that good samaritan ass dork is looking to make him do a bid. That wasn't part of the agreement. Sincere was supposed to walk and Tipton receives the time, remember?"

"That was never a guarantee, Rex. Sincere was caught with enough dope to shoot a fucking remake of the movie Boston George. This takes time and accurate facts. If I'm seen speaking with you in this parking lot. There's a possibility we could all be in the same prison by morning," Detective Sandra Elliot warned.

"I think you need to rephrase that because if I lose, you lose. That's a promise," Rex's voice grew a little louder.

"I said to let me handle my fucking business. You're not the only one who has threats and the deal is still running perfectly. Keep your lane and let me handle the rest," she ordered.

Rex smirked and turned the volume of his music to the max. The loudspeakers in his trunk rattled recklessly before he smashed off like a mad man.

Detective Sandra Elliot's heart pumped faster than a man on ten Viagra's. The thought of Rex knowing about her opposite plans would've placed a suicide rope around her second payment. The rain continued to dance on her skin and the meeting with Agent Witherspoon started to look very shaky. Her eyes fluttered while staring at the Parole building's entrance. Instead of continuing inside, she turned around and headed back for her car. Rex wasn't the only person with a trick up their sleeve and he was surely about to notice that shit very quickly.

***

After making it back to the house, Janita entered the front door and didn't expect everyone to be having a meeting in the center of her living room. The more shocking shit was seeing Peaches in the mix like she was actually trying help. Janita locked the front door and stood quietly.

Halo observed her expression and made his way over to her side. "Is something wrong, Goddess?"

"Yeah, it is. I spoke to Tipton last night, and I need to clear the air on a few things. I just need to know that you will stand behind me. The same way you support him? I can't do it alone," her tone was humble.

Halo could sense something was wrong. "Whatever you say, Goddess, I'm here," he guaranteed.

"Good." Janita walked over to Demon, Rika, Sonya, and Peaches. They all occupied the couch as if the smooth leather was gonna help them come up with a new idea on fixing the shitty problem at hand. "I know this might sound crazy, but I'm glad all of y'all here, right now. It shows that my husband has real supporters, and that means the world to me." Janita placed her hands behind her and took a deep breath.

"Yeah, that's sweet, but we've been sitting here since you've disappeared earlier. Ain't a damn thing changed, and this is getting more complicated by the second." Sonya folded her arms with an exhausted frown.

Janita nodded with understanding. "I know, but that's about to change. Last night when I was on the phone with Tipton. I realized that family is the only way to hold a bond and trust together. My husband is sitting behind the wall for the cause of my brother and Rex. That's not family behavior. So, I've come down to the conclusion, I'm taking over Tipton's business until further notice. Halo, if Sincere shows up to his court hearing in the morning and makes one remark. I want him dead within forty-eight hours. Everything will go through me and operate the same way it would as if Tipton was here himself. Rika, you said your product can still be purchased. Make it happen today. I'll let Halo gather the workers and use the best cookers to handle the business. The same goes for his out of state connections. If they owe money, continue to make them pay. If they disagree, we can make the necessary trips in the midst of getting Kimmi back."

"I support Tipton no matter how it comes. I'll get it done," Rika agreed with a confident nod.

"Good, this is a different step I'm making today. This is a day of strength to rebuild the foundation of the word family. If we're dealing with personal matters, it will only be handled by the hands of real loved ones. The few we can actually trust.

"What's gotten into you overnight girl? Did he give you some dick through the phone or something?" Sonya questioned with a raised brow. The new attitude was a turn on for a freaky motherfucker like herself.

"It's not the right time, Sonya." Janita disregarded her remark and faced Demon. "I'm not sure about what you have planned, but I'm sure if Tipton trusted you to do something, I can too. Protect us and follow the right people in order to find my husband's child."

"Yes ma'am, I will do my best indeed," Demon's voice clarified his vote about being on board with the rest.

Janita looked over at Peaches last and huffed. She cut her eyes at Halo and held out her hand. "Give me your gun, Halo."

Instead of questioning her request, he pulled his gun off the right side of his hip and placed it in Janita's hand. Her attention diverted back to Peaches who was now looking nervous as a motherfucker.

"I know me and you haven't gotten along since we've met and quite frankly it'll never work. I'm just dealing with you on the strength of my husband. So, I'll ask you once. Are you family or our enemy?" Janita held Halo's gun in her hand with a calm posture.

"First of all, you have a gun in your hand speaking about family. You might need to rephrase that, sweetie. If you're asking me where I stand with, my baby daddy. Just know we will always be family." Peaches smirked.

Janita knew her next move was the best move and the time for procrastination was over. She walked over to Peaches and swung her arm colliding the gun across her face. The loud smack quacked throughout the living room causing the others to look in shock. Peaches fell to the floor in a daze. The center of her head started to bleed profusely. Janita stood over her with the gun aimed for her head. "Now I'm gonna ask you again, bitch! We all family in here. Where is, Kimmi?"

Peaches stammered over her words, trying her best to shake the dizziness. "You stupid hoe! Why would I lie about my fucking daughter?" She was breathing erratically holding her face.

Janita removed her cellphone and started strolling down the text messages. Turning it around for Peaches to see, Janita mashed it close to her face. "What is this then, huh? You sent a message to Rex yesterday, but guess what dummy. You sent it to the wrong name."

Peaches looked at the phone with a sad expression. She tried to wipe the blood from her face to see.

Halo walked over to them and grabbed the phone from Janita's hand. Glancing at the message, he read it out loud, "Rex, you said that my daughter would be back in five days. This isn't what we agreed to, bring my baby."

After Halo finished reading the message. All eyes in the room rotated down to Peaches. Janita pulled the hammer on the gun back with a straight face. "I'll ask you again because family doesn't hurt family. Where in the fuck is my daughter cause she damn sure don't belong to you?"

The tears began to pour out of Peaches' eyes like faucets. Shaking her head, she gazed up at Janita. "I didn't think he was gonna take her for real. I just wanted the money, I swear."

"Halo, tie this bitch up," Janita spat with disgust.

"Hold up." Sonya stood from the couch with anger pumping from her chest. "You mean to tell me this lame ass bitch had her own baby snatched? We should just go ahead and kill her ass now." She pulled her gun slowly.

"I can't, this is Tipton's decision. I haven't explained anything to him yet. It's enough pressure with being in the holding facility so this drama would only make things worse. I'm gonna take care of it myself because Tipton isn't prepared to handle his business. This little cunt right here is our mission now," Janita confirmed as Halo quickly restrained Peaches.

"So, what the hell does this mean now? If this bitch got the baby, she knows the address where to find her," Sonya guessed.

"Well, that's where Demon comes in. I'm sure if she got an address for us, he can get it."

"The source is clearly right here in our face. I can make that bitch cough up that."

Janita waited until Halo was done to speak, "Trust me, she's in a position where it ain't no negotiating. Demon, do you mind if I borrow one of those little knives, please?"

Demon flashed Janita a wide grin and headed to retrieve his briefcase.

"I didn't hurt my daughter. It was just to get some money. I needed fucking money," Peaches cried and squirmed with nervousness.

Janita squatted down in front of her pathetic ass. "If I find out Kimmi's been hurt, even just a little. I'll make sure Tipton never hears about you again."

The statement caused her body to quiver in fear before Demon stepped back inside the living room.

Chapter 13
Rogers Federal Inmate Facility

As he headed out to his attorney visit, Tipton hoped that maybe some good news was now available. Word on the street was that the trap didn't eat without the numbers he was offering. Not to mention he was the best chef for the dope game to ensure all had a chance to make some bread. The update on Kimmi was still no better. So, even with all the money in the world, it still couldn't take away the stress about his daughter. He entered the small visiting booth, nodded at Wallace and took a seat in front of him.

"This is odd to show up when you know I have court tomorrow. I've been waiting for you." He folded his arms impatiently.

Wallace smiled. "Tipton, I can assure that I'm putting all things in order for you to win this thing. There are minor difficulties we will have, but the rest is piece of cake."

"What?"

"Sincere, the state wants to press for trial immediately if he comes and states that you were the one he was trafficking cocaine for. Now, this could work two ways. You go against him and he testifies. That'll be a very bad outcome. Now if he doesn't, I can guarantee you'll be walking out of that door with a smile big as Cherokee the pornstar's ass."

"So, Sincere is the only thing holding me back? What about Kenny Quick?" Tipton questioned with an inquisitive expression.

"Kenny will only be able to make a statement on things that doesn't hold weight. The only one who he's placed himself around is Sincere, not you. There is no history of transactions so that's not our worry. I'll rip him into pieces with one question."

Tipton nodded, but his expression told Wallace that he wanted to say more. The thought of Rex forced him to ask the buzzer. "So, did you ever find out how Sincere was caught up? If there's a witness who turned him in. We have the right to face him, right?"

Wallace nodded his head in approval. "Well, actually it's your right. We have the authority to cross-examine all witnesses and involved parties that mentioned your name."

"I want that information found out by morning. If we start trial, we're gonna be sure we know who we're up against," Tipton confirmed.

In the back of his head, he could see Rex's slimy ass face behind the act. It was easy to warn the cops about Sincere's movements when he was able to hear all the business of shipments and connections. The same way he took out Sleepy. He was pacing steps and using close ones as the pawns for his chessboard. Tipton wasn't dumb, and nothing could beat the cross, but the double.

Wallace placed a small discovery packet on the table in front of him. "You might wanna go over these few papers, right here. It's probably a few things you need to know in there. I'll be ready by morning. I'm fighting to get you home, it's my duty." He shook Tipton's hand sternly.

"I'm counting on you."

A moment of silence fell through the room and Tipton's eyes were glued to his with a firm message. There wasn't a such thing as losing. If he could make it through Sincere not touching the stand. The door to freedom would be one step closer.

***

The last few glares of sunlight were lowering below the horizon, while Halo sat outside of Tipton's house on the back patio. The thought of his friend suffering from the case made things worse with Kimmi being away. Pain was upon Tipton's family and Halo could feel the energy getting worse. Nothing would make him turn his back, especially when his child was still in the arms of an enemy.

Sonya stepped on the back porch, closing the door behind her. "Hey, luva." She sashayed over to him.

"What's up, Goddess?" Halo smiled as if all was well.

"That face you just had before I spoke to you, that's wassup. Are you okay?" She sat down gently on his lap and wrapped her arms around Halo's neck.

Her eyes were misty brown and Sonya's face always seemed to draw him in for a passionate kiss. Their lips locked and caressed one another. She felt so soft and innocent, Sonya's body would quiver in joy every time Halo placed his hands upon her.

"Why do you think I met you, Goddess?" His blue eyes stared into her soul. The question gave her a slight chill. Not from fear, but of not knowing a true answer.

"Truly Halo, I dont know. I've lived my life not knowing a lot of things, but I've learned to accept what comes and goes. I focus more on enjoying the moment, instead of living uptight and miserable until my last day. Maybe you're here to be a good dick I ride, or maybe you're here to actually sweep me off my feet for the long run. All I can do is wait patiently and see." Sonya smirked before staring off into the beautiful sky view.

"Do you wanna know why I'm here?" Halo asked.

"Yes."

"I'm here because I've always seen myself finding a place to call home. When I met, God. I knew it was meant for me to follow and see where the journey took me. My instincts led me to accept his invite on gaining success. I felt that whatever happened in the mix would be decreed. It was meant to meet, Tipton, you and his child. I'm here to make sure she gets back because the one who kept his promise to me isn't in the same position as when we first started. I respect God's wife like a sister. So, I'm willing to stand behind her until the end. It's obviously the same duty we all got," his words trailed off as if he was visioning a victory for them all.

"Why do you call him, God?" Sonya stared down at her mystery man with a straight face.

"I've went my entire life knowing that God exists, but I still have yet to see. At a certain point, I felt there was no such thing. The heartless world and circle we called family showed me. I grew to think that emotions powered people instead of a heart, a mind to know when something is wrong, or right. I never saw it until I met him. His honesty, the mind to know right from wrong. The actions of caring and showing it, instead of speaking on it. All the characteristics, the supreme being wanted us to see, and imply. God has it. I gave him that name to believe that great people do live on this earth, and maybe the high one just creates destruction, because it's natural for all of us. He's the reason I kept hope."

"I respect that, Halo. He helped you. I'm down with the fact of you riding hard for a cause you really stand on. But the same way he gave you motivation. The supreme being gave you life to pursue that same energy. You've never seen him, but you believe. The same way you breathe and know that air exists, but you still can't see it. You can't touch it. That's the proof, Halo. No man can create that. Not even, Tipton. I hope that this journey leads you to where you really wanted to be because I'm surely happy to say I met you. I bet Tipton does, too. Ask yourself who does he give thanks to for that?" Sonya pointed her index finger in the air. She placed another kiss on his lips and rose from his lap. "Speaking of riding with Tipton's queen to the end, she's calling for you. I'm guessing she has it all figured out on what's next. Do you truly trust following her word with this?" Sonya wanted to see if Halo's mind was seeing the outcome.

"I really do, Goddess is in love. Her passion for him won't let her fail. I can see it in her eyes. She's not gonna stop until all this is back right. I support her for that reason," Halo replied.

"Good, because that new bad girl shit, she's pulling, right now is real sexy. I think I like this, Janita." Sonya giggled with a devilish smile.

Chapter 14
7.45 a.m.

The wind was pumping heavy and the sun was beaming hard as ever. Janita tightened her slim Chanel peak coat, before handing Halo a set of car keys for the rented Dodge Avenger. "It's all set, you'll know when I send the text."

"I got you, Goddess." He wasted no time heading down the parking lot.

Sonya slapped Janita's butt lightly with a smile. "I like the way you stepping up, baby girl. Show them this your shit." She winked and headed for her own car.

Janita shook her head and moved back over to Rika. "All you have to do is watch that bitch. She's in the closet and shouldn't come out for any reason. I should be back right after Tipton's hearing."

"Understood," Rika stated calmly before walking back into the residence.

Janita watched her until she reached the front door. The vibes must have been mutual because Rika turned to lock eyes with her before closing the front door. The action didn't stop Janita from keeping the business-focused first. The smallest shit could ruin it, and that small problem was Rika getting her ass beat for trying to play the role.

Hoping in Tipton's Mclaren, she headed straight for the courthouse. It took a minute to slide pass all the early morning traffic, but it didn't take over twenty minutes to reach the Federal courthouse that sat in the center of Downtown Atlanta. She looked her watch, she was ten minutes early, and that would only be enough time to get inside and find Wallace. Janita parked, made her way through the front entrance and went through the proper motions in order to pass the front desk. By the time she made her way to the fourth floor. Tipton's lawyer Wallace was stepping out of the courtroom doors. His eyes landed on Janita and headed straight for her.

"Mrs. White, I'm not sure if we were on the same page when we spoke last night? But it seems like your brother is here and he's prepared to get on the stand against Tipton if need be."

"Don't worry about him, continue," she ordered before he could finish the statement.

"But, Mrs. White?"

"Wallace, court is about to start." Janita held open the entrance door waiting for him to proceed.

"Right away, Mrs. White."

Trailing inside, Janita found her section on the second bench as Wallace made his way to the defendant and attorney's desk. The timing was perfect because the judge was approaching and the cases were about to officially began.

"All rise for the Honorable Judge Leazer," a bald head ass bailiff stepped up and called out loudly.

Of course, the entire room rose beside Janita. Her mind was only tied on Tipton. After the fake ass introduction. The judge opened his calendar. "It's good to see you all this morning. I'm hoping we can get started pretty quick with this load. My first case will be the state vs Tipton White. Wallace step forward."

Your honor, I'm Mr. White's representative. His wife is also in attendance today."

"Great, we can proceed." The judge nodded to his two sheriffs. They dispersed through a small side door and reappeared a few minutes later with Tipton in shackles.

Janita's eyes locked on to her love and instantly wanted to cry. Through all of his bad luck, he still looked good as ever, but his bruised bottom lip stated that he was involved in a little more than just doing time. He was only gone a few weeks and everything about his aura stated that he'd became even stronger. His eyes met hers and flashed that handsome ass smile. Janita's kitty purred in delight, every step he made, she matched his gaze until they seated him.

Judge Leazer flipped through a few documents in front of him before eyeing the District attorney. "So, what does the state have?"

The blonde-haired, white man stood to his feet with a charming smile. "Your honor, the state has been doing an undercover investigation on the defendant for a while now. We've taken the proper procedures and investigated thoroughly for the charges that are being brought up against Mr. White today. He has two conspiracy charges and one drug trafficking with possession. The day his home was raided they found five kilo wrappings sitting by the toilet in his upstairs bedroom. It's clear that Mr. White is a drug kingpin. We have a witness who is willing to testify on behalf of this man's actions. Someone who actually isn't afraid of this man's power."

Sincere eyes moved over until they met Tipton's. The coldness in his eyes could be felt from across the room. This was the moment he could never replay. Turning his attention to the judge, he cleared his throat. "I can verify things more briefly your honor. I'm willing to testify if necessary." Sincere swallowed his spit and the air suddenly began to thicken in the room. He turned to look behind him. Janita's glare sent shivers down his spine. Her eyebrows were slanted with hatred, but the calm posture she carried was starting to make him more nervous.

"Well, if this is true what you speak of. What does the defendant have to say about this?" the judge questioned impatiently.

Wallace stood to his feet quickly. "Judge Leazer, this is ridiculous. They found a few kilo wrappings of planted evidence. We still haven't received the results back for that. This guy right here, their second witness," Wallace stated while pointing at Agent Witherspoon. "Better known as, Kenny Quick. He has not one record of ever meeting with my client for drug dealings. Only the so-called star witness here. He's been the direct contact for these operations, and my client is being dragged into this with a blind eye."

"That's bull." The District attorney jumped from his seat. "Your honor, this man is oblivious to his client's actions. We have witnesses, and they have the right to bring this man to justice for cross-examination."

"By law, the state would be correct. If we have more than one witness. The process of the trial would have to be placed into effect. If the evidence of the kilo wrappings tests out to be negative. I'll grant bond. Until then, I'm gonna have to put Mr. White on hold," Judge Leazer banged his gavel.

Wallace waved his arms around like a mad man. "Your Honor that's absurd. You haven't even heard my client's qualities. He's a husband with a child and the sole provider of his family. He only has one prior on his record and that time was served."

"And what prior would that be Mr. Wallace?" Judge Leazer exhaled.

"It was just a mishap of aggravated assault, he was a minor."

"That mishap was a school shooting that led to someone shot, and others injured from the stampedes of kids running for their lives. He endangered the entire neighborhood fleeing from the scene and hiding out until late that night. He then turned himself in your honor," the district attorney explained, then clapped his hands together and smirked with amusement. "He's a killer also your honor. This is a federal case, not an armed robbery of a local corner store. This guy is smuggling bricks of cocaine in the United States, sir. That's our proof and we're prepared to start trial immediately. The state has nothing else to say." He sat back down and rubbed a hand through his smooth, blonde hair.

"Mr. Wallace, a school shooting is serious. Maybe you should prepare your case, and let's see exactly who this young man is. I'm sorry, Mr. Wallace. This first appearance will be carried over. I'll set a date for three weeks, that's final," Judge Leazer dismissed any further request.

Sincere was escorted out first, his guilty ass face was glued to the ground and the district attorney shook his hand with joy. Janita watched them all walk out as if he didn't just throw her husband to the wolves.

The bailiffs grabbed Tipton and lifted him from the seat. He looked at Janita and blew her a kiss. "It'll be okay, just stay focused." He smiled before they walked him behind the court doors.

Janita soaked his words in and was sure not to drop a tear. After she calmly texted Halo's phone. Wallace walked over to her and placed a copy of Tipton's discovery packet in her hand.

"He wanted me to give you these. He said once you read them, you will know what to do. I'm going to prepare for his trial to make sure we can get him home. There's nothing else that we can do."

Janita forced a smile as she stood to her feet. "There's always other avenues Wallace." She turned on her heels and left the courtroom.

Making her way back down to the first floor, she exited through the glass doors and released her stream of tears. It was hard to hold the pain. Tipton begged her not to let the opponents see her sweat and the barrier was so close to breaking after he was led back through that dark ass door. The pain hurt twice as much for the next step she was about to take. Tipton's life was going to be protected by any means, even if close pieces had to be removed. The Queen was only meant for one position, to protect her King. She reached the parking deck, climbed inside Tipton's McLaren, and started the engine. She used her cell to place another call.

The line ringed three times before a male's voice answered, "Who's speaking?"

"I'm ready, you can proceed with it," Janita responded.

The line was silent for a few seconds. "Consider it done ma'am," the man agreed to her request and ended the call.

Janita tossed her phone aside, backed out of her space, and smashed through the small lot. Now, was the time for her plan to go into effect. Tipton's life depended on it, and him coming home wasn't going to be an option. Whatever it took, however necessary.

Chris Green

Chapter 15

It didn't take longer than thirty minutes for Janita to get home after dropping off some more money for Tipton's legal representation. Wallace was surely in need of help if he was trying to fuck with the crooked ass district attorney. Instead of waiting, she purchased the best lawyers for drug cases in the state of Georgia. Once that was secured, she focused on the payment that was due for Rex. Today was the time limit for the second meet up, Janita wanted to be extra positive on how to play things out. She spotted Halo's rental after pulling up through the driveway of her home. After parking her car, she killed the engine and headed inside.

Once her foot stepped inside the folds of her home. Sincere's eyes grew wide. The left side of his face was severely swollen and a sock muffled his screams. The sight of him didn't put any sympathy on her heart. Halo held the back of his neck with a firm grip and Janita decided to get the hard part out of the way. She walked over to her brother flashing him a disappointed look when his eyes downcast. Halo snatched the sock from his mouth.

"I didn't mean to sis. It was just to protect you. He's going to get you killed." Sincere was trying to breathe.

"You didn't do anything to protect me, Sincere. Because if you did, you would have stood beside my husband, not against him. The thought of you even introducing me to him causes pain that I can't explain. Don't you understand that you're the reason he's sitting in there?" Janita looked down at him pathetically.

"I'm not the only reason," he admitted.

Pondering on his comment, she disapproved by shaking her head. "You were supposed to keep it, family, overall. What you did was disloyal, after everything my husband did for you. There is no shame in snitching on the one who made your way, huh? Do you even realize how bad this has destroyed my family."

Her rhetorical question forced him to think, but nothing seemed to escape his lips, not even a small apology. Sincere really crossed balances with his deadly mistake and before shit crumbled, he knew no one would forgive him. He coughed roughly, but Halo continued to hold his head straight.

"If you think I'm the only one, Janita, you're wrong!" Sincere shouted with a shaky tone.

"No, you're wrong for what you did. That's what you wanted. Does it even make you feel a little bad?" Janita questioned, her tone delivery expressed that she was more hurt than mad.

Sincere took a deep breath, the pain of his swollen face pulsated horribly. "I'm sorry, sis. This ain't what it looks like, Janita. I'm your brother. I'm sorry, but they made me do it. I can't go to prison. I really love you, Janita. You're my flesh and blood." His chest heaved at a fast pace.

Janita mustered a small smile as a tear dropped down her cheeks. "Good." She looked up at Halo before walking away.

She headed for the back porch, stepped outside and eased her tension. The feeling of Sincere's deceit was clawing at her emotions, but the new mission was already in effect. It was too late to turn around.

Boom! The loud gun roaring from inside the home forced her to slightly flinch. She closed her eyes, inhaled the fresh air and allowed that hard burden to be released from her system, it was over. She opened the small Manila envelope Wallace had provided her with earlier. She scanned the few sheets of paper until coming across the witness list, her mouth widened in shock.

Halo captured her vision through the back door. He walked over to her and lowered his head. "It's done, Goddess."

"Good, alert Rex for the second payment. This time it's on me," she requested calmly.

Choices had to be made and there wasn't anymore time for meltdowns to be held in the middle. When the innocent remained humble, they become prey. The establishment was already enforced, it needed to be respected. Janita was gonna be the one to make it happen. After Halo filled her in on Tipton's ties and instructions for the operation. She took action, in order to get Kimmi back things would have to play exactly the way Demon mapped out. Like a game of monopoly.

***

Two Hours Later

After arriving back at the facility, the transferring officer parked and pulled Tipton from out of the back seat. Before the rookie guard could release him from the cuffs. An elderly white Captain enforcer stopped them in their tracks.

"Excuse me, Mr. Kelson. Where is this inmate coming from?" he questioned the guard.

"Good evening, Cap. He's back from court. I'm going to pick up the next load and process this one back in."

"No need, I'll handle his process. You can go ahead and finish your routes," he interfered and walked Tipton inside of the building himself.

As they entered the booking area, the old man walked him in the opposite direction of his assigned dorm. Tipton's eyebrow raised in curiosity before asking the quiet man of authority, "Uh, excuse me, Sir. Is this a trip to medical or something? I'm in building-C. My dorm is that way."

"Not anymore, now shut the fuck up," he spoke with a distasteful tone.

"What?"

"You heard me, motherfucker. I'm running the show here, not you. One more word and you'll be munching on salami sandwiches for breakfast, lunch and dinner, son."

He jerked Tipton down the narrow hallway, it led to a small steel door. After the Captain radioed for the entrance to be popped. The medal frame buzzed allowing them to pass through. The dorm was quiet on the inside and bars wrapped around the windows of the inmate cell doors.

Tipton looked around the solitary building and snapped. "Wait, what the fuck am I doing here?"

The man walked him over to cell twenty-six and activated the steel door to open. He released Tipton from the cuffs and forced him to step inside the filthy room. "I'll introduce myself so we can come to a better understanding, Mr. White. I'm Captain Two Fucks which means I could give a rat's ass about your attitude, or problems. Welcome to the death box of confinement. You will be here until your private investigation is over. If you make my job hard, I'll destroy your entire bid here, son. Stay off my door and mind your manners. The rest will flow smoother than a cow shitting on grass," he stated before slamming the door in Tipton's face.

The smell of urine and burned cigarettes roamed inside the cell. The toilet was dark black and looked as if it wasn't used in months. Tipton walked over to the sealed window. He searched for any sign of light. There was no sign of movement and the hole was quieter than a cemetery around three in the morning. He took a seat on the bunk. Tipton was sure not to touch anything.

His property and mat were left back in the building. His mind pondered on what the hell occurred for him to be placed in the box. Sincere was probably half of the reason. Not too many people were able to handle a close friend testifying against them in the court of law. It usually led to someone being murdered, or even a victim committing suicide. Tipton leaned back on the bed, rested his eyes, and thought about Kimmi. She needed her dad, but it was becoming harder to see that happen with the pressure on his back.

He just wanted the pain to stop, Tipton needed his freedom. He raised off the bed, got on his knees and did something he truly wasn't used to doing, *Prayed.*

Chapter 16
9:30 p.m.

Rex stood in the center of the Lowes warehouse parking lot waiting for Halo to arrive with his money. The designated time that was set had passed, and there was still no sign of him appearing to complete his end of the deal. He looked down at his watch and blew out a deep breather in aggravation. Traffic was flowing smoothly throughout the section, and it was no excuse for the disrespectful action of leaving him looking stupid if this was going to be a no show. Just when he was about to call and deliver his threatening message. Tipton's black McLaren pulled swiftly inside of the parking space. The headlights shined on Rex forcing him to raise his hand.

His heart pace increased causing a hand to reach for the pistol on his hip. Instead of seeing Halo step out of the driver's seat, Janita opened the car door and spit the bubblicious gum from her mouth. Her Gucci pumps touched the ground allowing Janita to rise and flaunt her beautiful body. The fitted Versace dress gripped her tighter than a fiend sucking a pipe. Her hair was pulled back in two pigtails and the make up she wore looked as if her next stop was the Nicki Minaj pink print tour. She was better than magnificent, she was astounding. Every word that coincided with the elite. Rex stared in amazement until she closed the small space and stood in front of him.

"Janita?" He stepped forward until he could smell the apple lotion pumping off her skin.

"That's my name," she said sarcastically while looking around with a tedious expression.

"You looking good I see." Rex raised his eyebrow in amazement. His eyes couldn't help but glance at that ass. "Uh, is there any reason the blue eye dragon's not here? I think you came to the wrong meeting, sweetie."

Janita yawned. "I'm at the right meeting, Rex. This is my show after all."

Rex couldn't help but laugh before wiggling his finger. "That was funny. Like Tipton is really dumb enough to let you do something so stupid. Seriously, where is this punk ass nigga with my dough?"

Shaking her head, Janita strolled to the back of her car and popped the trunk. She pulled the Michael Kors duffle bag from inside, then she walked back over to him and tossed the bag to his feet. "There you go, sir. Two hundred and fifty, all honchos."

Rex smirked, grabbed the bag and checked to be sure. He raised his eyes to meet hers, Janita smiled. "Is there something I'm missing? When did you become the sponsor for this business?" His serious face was on.

"When Tipton decided to be an ass and leave me. Things don't stop because he's facing life. Money has to be made, besides he's gonna need someone to keep those commissary books filled while facing thirty." Janita shrugged.

"So, let me get this straight." Rex raised a finger. "You mean to tell me little ole Nita has stepped up and taken over a drug empire? Do you even know anything about this shit?"

"I know enough, especially numbers. You shouldn't have to worry. You have every coin of your business request. That's what it's about, right? So, let me be the clueless suburban girl who doesn't know anything. I think that I do it well." She grinned before shifting her hips to the right.

Rex was glued on her beauty. Her eyelids even blinked with confidence, and the new appearance was causing him to grow slightly stiff just from speaking back and forth to her. He pushed closer to her and looked down into her eyes. She didn't budge, neither did she flinch from the sight of his gun handle.

"You know something, Nita. This game needs a bad one like you. Maybe you need the right push, and you could run this shit yourself. You wouldn't need, Tipton. His business would become yours, I respect you more than him." He smirked while glancing down at her cleavage.

"Is that so?"

"Yeah, it is. See your man don't respect the game. I don't know if I can say the same for you. It looks like you're a boss bitch to me. Especially standing right here in front of me when this serious ass shit going down between us. That's gangsta." He pushed a layer of Janita's hair from her face.

Janita laughed, then she eyed him up and down before taking a step back. "I don't care what Tipton thinks. I'm the breadwinner, right now. So, that means my rules matter, nothing else. I'm not sure how long you're willing to play this game for his little child. I can easily give you the money to end this. We know Tipton can't fight a war with you, well I know. This would be better if you give back the little brat. I can be able to get him off my back and do what I please in peace." Janita played with her nails nonchalantly.

"Really, what happened to the whole husband thing. You mean to tell me all that support and love was fake?" Rex questioned her loyalty.

"Never, the loyalty will always be there, sir. But life moves on, I have to survive for me, enjoy me. I'm willing to do anything for my spot, but as I said it'll be easier if you place the kid out of this subject. I can at least feel better about my dealings if I get Kimmi back. I owe him that, nothing else."

"Anything, huh?" Rex rubbed down the side of her hip.

Janita stared at his finger with a sharp eye. She popped his hand down. "Please don't touch. Maybe you'll understand the game also. You can't have the cake and eat it also, Rex. Let's try working on the kid first. Then we can communicate a little better. You shouldn't be so anxious to fuck your best friend's wife, should you?" She giggled before walking back to the car. Their eyes met before she got in and pulled calmly off the scene.

Rex smiled thinking about the new fresh opportunity. The thought of having Tipton's spot placed a light of joy in his sneaky ass head. It was the game of fitness. The laws of winning without breaking a sweat. Now that the rules were being followed. '*It's time to boost it up a notch,*' he thought before climbing in his whip to leave.

Chris Green

***

Arriving back to her home, Janita stepped out of her car to find Halo waiting in the parking lot pacing in circles. His attention rotated straight to her before she could enter the house. "Are you okay, Goddess? Did he touch you?" He noticed the unpleasant look on her face.

"No, Halo, I'm okay, but we have to be clear on what's about to happen. I need to apply more pressure and he's gonna abide. He's weak," she informed him before they walked inside of the crib.

She spotted Rika standing in the living room on her cell. Janita flashed a frown. The gesture caused her to hang up the call and take a seat on the couch. Her curly red dreadlocks were wrapped in a ponytail and the one-piece jumper she wore made her figure stand out like a sore thumb.

"If you don't mind could you please put some clothes on in my home?" Janita asked with a demanding tone.

Rika obliged but shook her head before heading off to the guest room.

"Goddess, Sonya, and Demon have been on post for the past three hours, and we've seen the same movements. It's probably best if we make a move now. Kimmi could be in one of these locations," Halo suggested.

"Not yet, we need more foundation. It's easy to lose if we move off impulse. It's time to make the trips and set it in place. Demon has to finish the process, and the rest will fall accordingly. It's a domino effect and we need all the info before we can take action," Janita said as she walked to the hallway closet and opened it.

Peaches jumped in fear with wide eyes. Her hands and feet were taped to the chair and her face was still covered in dried up blood. After discovering the position she played in Kimmi's kidnapping, her ass couldn't be trusted, not for one second. Janita didn't spare her any mercy. The meals would be bread and water twice a day. Her pants would be her personal bathroom and judging from the flies, and horrible smell lingering in the small box. She definitely had taken a shit on herself.

Janita grabbed the bridge of her nose and turned her head in disgust. "Stinky ass bitch!" She removed the sock from Peaches' mouth. Janita showed her Tipton's paperwork she received from Wallace. "It's mighty funny that you don't know shit about my husband being arrested when you're on his witness list, Peaches. You sure there ain't nothing else we need to know?"

Her voice was shaky and the small torture was starting to break her ass in like a badass child that needed discipline. "I'm-uh—I don't want him to lose. I just wanted the money. Rex—" The hard, back slap from Janita's hand-cut her words off quickly. "Pleaseeee!" Peaches cringed in fear. "I can fix it, I'll help," her tone was desperate.

"How bitch, I wanna know?"

"There's a lady who was working with, Rex. I seen her the day he came to pick up, Kimmi. She was following behind him in a black car." Peaches shivered while spilling the beans.

"What's her name?"

"Umm, I can't reme—" Another slap put some sense in her dome a lot fucking faster. "Sandra, he said that Sandra would make sure we all get paid, she's knows, I swear." Peaches nodded her head repeatedly.

"Sandra?" Janita folded her arms with a curious face. "You mean, Sandra Elliot?"

"I'm not sure, I just know it's Sandra." Her head lowered with embarrassment.

Rika appeared from around the corner with an aggravated face. "You know, I've been quiet since arriving here because I know that this is your show Janita, but don't you think this is going too far. If she's agreeing to help, you maybe need to have a little more patience and see how we can go about handling this. Beating her will only make it worse."

Janita looked back at Halo like the comment maybe could've been for him. Watching his sight lower to the floor. She turned back to face Rika. "I'm sensing some type of energy, right now. Is that a sound of someone stating that I'm doing things wrong?"

"I'm just saying, I don't think Tipton would approve of us doing this. He moves strategically. All the chaos going on wouldn't be if he was here. Maybe you should try a different approach." Rika pointed at Peaches trembling in the closet.

"Tipton this, Tipton that. Every time I hear you come from your mouth, it's about my fucking husband. You know what's funny, ever since you've been here. That's all you've been able to speak on, Tipton. Is there anything you need to tell me?" Rika remained quiet until Janita stepped in her face. "I said is there anything you need to tell me? We don't have to play stupid. Have you ever fucked my man, Rika?"

Instead of being humble, Rika decided to lay the cards out. Refusing to let the young girl shine on her, she told the truth. "No, I've never fucked, Tipton. But I have sucked his dick numerous of times. What's even crazier is the fact of me actually having that chance if he didn't love you so much. He doesn't want me. All he speaks on is the life you and him will share after this life was over, and that leaves me nowhere, but alone with a bunch of unsold product. Maybe you should appreciate that often, instead of complaining. That man loves you but running and torturing all the close ones next to him will only create more friction. Maybe you feel like I'm out to get you, or maybe it's your insecurities eating at your head about not being the right one for a man who deals drugs. Regardless of how you feel you're Tipton's wife and I respect that. That's the only thing that matters," Rika admitted before walking off from her.

The statement caused Janita's heart to slightly ache. Tipton was so discreet with the way he carried himself that she never expected the answer to fly from Rika's mouth. The caged anger inside said to beat her into a fucking coma, but the uncut realness as a woman wouldn't allow her too. Not only did she admit to what she did but verified that it still couldn't replace the love Tipton shared for her as his wife. It didn't brighten the secret, but it explained the reason for her sincere loyalty. Rika was the same one to help Tipton rise when he arrived home from prison, and that was enough to prove what level she stood on with him.

Janita turned to face Halo and flashed a look of disappointment. Something told her that he knew about Tipton's little affair. Not wanting to stir the drama anymore. She decided to focus on the plan. "I need you to call, Sonya and tell her that we're heading out tomorrow. Demon and Rika will remain here until we return. The plane leaves early in the morning, so rest lightly," Janita ordered before shutting the closet door on Peaches' face.

She turned the opposite way to head upstairs, made it to the master bedroom and locked herself inside. As she took a seat on the bed, her mind pondered on walking back downstairs to blow Rika's brain across the living room mantelpiece. The thought of Tipton stepping out on her scarred deeply, but the thought of knowing his lifestyle forced her to remember that he was the charming guy she wanted. The one who she decided to be with forever. It was a lot that came with a man of his caliber, and that would take a while to adjust to. Still, after Rika's honesty, her love couldn't pump any lesser for the man she adored with a passion.

His touch alone would force her into submission. His mind, the captivating feeling of all his unique passion for pleasing her each time they connected as one. He was the only thing she had left to breathe and fight for. Sincere couldn't stop her loyalty, neither could a bitch who claimed to blow his dick like a lollipop. Tipton would remain the main key overall because he was meant to be in that spot. Kimmi meant the world to him as a father and Janita were next in line when it came down to family. She couldn't let him down, her words were bond and that shit was for life.

Chris Green

Chapter 17
11:30 p.m.

Detective Sandra Elliot couldn't help but smile after hearing the doorbell ring. After gaining all her evidence against Rex and Tipton. She was ready to put the press down on the judge to get them both a football number in prison. The money that was Rex was giving her made up for the back end of her troubles, but it wasn't enough to lose her career over. Thinking about the takeout she ordered. Her fingers snapped lightly until the door came open. The cold silenced pistol that connected with her forehead forced her to raise her hands in the air. She stared the white man in his face, as she kept her composure. He backed her inside the home, politely closing the door behind him.

The words trailed off his tongue with authority, "I need you to place your hands behind your head and cross your legs."

"Is this some type of robbery? Because I'm letting you know that it will not end well, buddy. You can just leave now if money is what you want."

Ignoring her threats, he placed two zip ties around her ankles and wrists. Making sure they were tight. He kicked her over forcing her to fall face-first on the floor.

"Son of a bitchhh!" she groaned in pain from his foot connecting to her head.

Taking off his jacket Demon tossed it on the couch and pulled a pair of vise grips from his waistline. Her face screwed up in fear, but she refused to show any weakness. "What is this about? I'm telling you that I'm an active Detective and if you touch me this will not be the last of it." She softened up as he got closer.

"It's okay ma'am, I'm only here for one reason. To make sure you're taken care of about your personal dealings. That's all."

"I don't know what you're talking about. What dealings? I have no dealings," she stressed looking up at him from the floor.

"Well, of course, you do Detective Elliot, Tipton." Demon grinned before caving the utensil into her mouth and snatching out her tongue within seconds.

"Aaaggghhhh! Aaaggghhhh!" she hollered with a horrible mumble as the blood began to pour quickly from her mouth. Her body was jerking back and forth like a fish that needed water.

Demon pulled a small piece of paper and crayon from his pocket. He kneeled beside her. "We're gonna play a little game of guess. For every question you answer wrong, I'll cut off an ear, finger, or toe whichever one you choose. My question is very easy," Demon taunted, clamping the pliers over and over.

Detective Sandra Elliot shook with a fearful expression, her mouth was closed tightly trying to keep the blood contained but laying on her stomach caused it to spill out.

"All I want to know is one thing. Where is, Rex?" Demon inquired with an unmerciful smirk.

The fear was crawling slowly down the back of her neck and just from the sound of his voice, she knew that making it out alive was probably a slim chance to none.

***

Los Angeles, California

11 ½ Hours Later

Stepping out of the black SUV, Janita looked over at Kima's mansion and nodded. "I'm sure that she has no problem paying with a house like this."

"Yeah, she's really not bad, especially if you know how to tame a coochie with your tongue game." Sonya snickered before heading quickly up the steps to her front porch. To their surprise, Tipton's men were first to answer the door and allow them access to Kima's home.

"Is there anything we need to worry about?" Janita said as they stepped through the threshold of her home.

"No, unless she acts dumb, then yes." Sonya waved her hand not caring what it turned out to be.

Janita shook her head. The ladies walked through the main hallway and bumped into Kima coming around the corner with six of her own crew members. "Uh, excuse me, Sonya. What are you doing here? My dues have been paid. And who the hell is this?" She nodded toward Janita with a nasty facial expression.

Before Sonya could respond Janita stepped forward. "My name's Janita, I'm Tipton's wife." She held out her hand delicately.

Accepting her gesture, Kima rolled her neck still in confusion. "Well, that's good that Tipton has pussy at home. He's so tight that I began to think the was fucking gay. Why are you here in my home is the grand question?" she responded.

Janita looked at all the sissy ass guards behind her. Most of the men looked like some shit straight out of good times, or maybe some niggas from back in the day when the police couldn't do shit but beat you half to death with a nightstick. These guys couldn't be taken serious. Most of Tipton's men entered the home to get a close ear on the meeting at hand.

"Look, Kima, you may not get it at the moment, but it's a process. Right now, I'm running the business for my husband, and I still will collect all the debts personally now. However, we are in need of assistance, and I was figuring, maybe we could work something out to gain a mutual understanding," Janita said with great respect.

"*Mutual understanding*? Bitch your husband has been taking my money from me ever since the first trip he made to L.A. This ain't nothing new. So, what the hell is you trying to work out? Cause it seems like you already got enough." Kima wouldn't allow anymore press to be paid without standing ground. Tipton was collecting over four-hundred grand from her territory within two weeks. It was more than extortion. He was trying to put her out of business.

Sonya cut her eyes at Janita wondering if she was about to accept the backtalk from the scary hoe. Just when Sonya was about to speak, Janita stopped her again. "Listen, Kima, this will make it clear for you. It's two options, I need your help with something in Georgia. If you will allow me to carry a few of your men with me.

I'll be sure that everyone returns unharmed, and I will also remove my men from your territory."

"What about the debt?" Kima folded her arms.

"I'll clear it off, and deal with Tipton on my end."

"And what if I don't agree?"

"Then I'll shoot you in your head and kill you in front of everybody, right now." Janita pulled the pistol slowly from her lower back.

Tipton shooters were clutching hard in case one of her weak ass heroes caught a bright one in the head. There was not gonna be any debating, Janita was ready to prove it. The two women held eye contact while Janita gripped the gun tightly.

Sonya stepped forward and touched Kima's shoulder, before whispering in her ear, "Please, just take the deal. It's the only way you can slide away from this for good."

It didn't take long to think after Janita said she was willing to remove her men and allow her trap spots to flow back to normal. Kima held out her hand. Janita smiled and embraced her gesture. "Thank you, Kima. It'll only be a few days."

"Yeah, whatever. Can y'all please stop barging in my shit, and warn me before coming unannounced? That definitely doesn't show respect. Take the men you need and exit that way." Kima pointed with a smirk.

Sonya looked her up and down with a freaky smile, as Janita turned to leave. "Maybe I'll be back alone, Kima. Is that okay?"

"I don't want yo' ass, Sonya. You need to find another bitch to fuck on, baby girl, 'cause it ain't me."

"Yeah, right, girl I'll beat yo ass." Sonya laughed before bumping pass all the scary-ass bodyguards. She could tell from the way Kima responded, that her kitty was definitely still wrapped in a hot pocket.

Making her way outside with Janita, Sonya climbed inside the car. "So, what are we doing now?"

"The same thing I told you yesterday. We need all the help we can get, Sonya. We will not be able to match these people if we ain't got enough supporters backing us. It's the only chance we have left." Janita glanced out of the window of her truck.

"So, how we coming? Is these dudes rolling or what?"

Janita stared at all the men who waited for her call on what to do. "They're needed and I can't take the chance on not bringing them."

"So, what are you saying? How many do we need? It's like forty-eight guys here, Janita." Sonya waved her hand around at all the security.

"All of them," she demanded.

Sonya laughed until she realized that Tipton's crazy-ass wife was dead serious. Putting the funny energy to the side, she shrugged her shoulders. "Fuck it." She raised out of the backseat and yelled to all the men who stood around. "All you fellas let's load it up. We heading back home. Let's go, let's go," she commanded.

The movement of the men began to shuffle as they mounted up in the parked suburbans. Sonya smiled at how easy it was to make some shit shake. "If an army is what you want, you got it, sister." She closed the door and tapped the driver's shoulder to pull off.

"Yes." Janita nodded. "If things go right with Halo in Omaha. We will be able to head home tonight. When we arrive in the city, everyone needs to make it to their section, and lay low until the time comes."

Sonya smirked. "All you have to do is let me handle that, baby girl. This is what you have me for."

"Good." Janita smiled before pulling out her line to call Halo.

Chris Green

Chapter 18

Halo stepped out of his black 2019 Tahoe and walked in the parking lot of Milo's new mini-mansion. Ever since Tipton got arrested, his status flamed through the roof. Money was being made from every angle and Tipton's armed security team was making sure to multiply with every corner they began to slang on. A few men watched as Halo entered the parking space, gun in hand. By the time he reached the front door. Tipton's entire security team was mounted behind him.

"Yo', Halo, is there a new agenda or something?" one of the shooters stepped to the front and asked.

"Just pay attention," he replied.

As he walked through the large home, Halo moved until he reached the living room. Milo sat on a huge suede couch with a Gracia Vega hanging from his lips. His posture changed upon seeing the killer step inside the room.

"Halo, what the hell are you doing here man?" He stood up nervously?"

"I came to negotiate, Milo. We need to talk, now," he replied before taking a seat.

"Talk about what? We got an understanding already, my dude. You got the paper for this week. Is there a problem?" Milo asked confused.

"Tipton is in a bind. We have a problem on our hand. So, I will need to borrow a few of your men to ride down to Atlanta with me," Halo stated calmly.

"What, Atlanta? There's nothing down in the city for my team. You can just carry these niggas who you left in my shit with you, and that's your group, right there. Shit is moving in Omaha for me, Halo. I can't allow them to leave, because that leaves me vulnerable." Milo gave him a stupid look.

Before Halo could reply, his phone began to ring. He pulled it from his coat pocket, spotted Janita's name and quickly answered. "I'm here, Goddess."

"Halo, is Milo agreeing to our terms?" Janita questioned.

"I'm in the process, right now, Goddess. There might be a small issue," he informed her while looking at Milo.

"Can you please let me speak with him?"

Halo stood off the couch to pass him the phone. Milo hesitated on grabbing the line at first but decided to see what the hell was up Tipton's sleeve. "Who is this?"

"Hi, Milo, this is Janita. I'm sure you may know my husband and unfortunately, he's not able to handle this conversation, right now. So, I'm filling in, if Halo has explained to you what's going on. I would really like for you to cooperate. If that is possible, I will return the favor with removing my husband's soldiers from your territory. It'll squash all ties," Janita offered.

Milo looked at the phone recklessly. "Listen, whatever your name is again. Just like I told him, that can't happen. That's gonna place me in a predicament that I'm not willing to go through for the sake of you, or your man. Bad enough y'all already got niggas moving directly in my shit. That's enough," he stressed through the receiver.

"Thank you, Milo. Can you please give the phone back to Halo now?"

Chuckling, he tossed the cell back to Halo. "Obviously, it's a misunderstanding, bro."

Instead of taking his word, Halo placed his ear to the touchscreen. "Hello?"

"Halo, Milo is not understanding," Janita stated with a hint of aggravation.

"Whatever you say, Goddess." He hung up the phone and placed it back into his coat pocket. Then stood to his feet. He shrugged his shoulders. "A'ight, Milo, I'll holla at you later." Halo removed his pistol and placed a slug between his eyes before he could reject it. His hand raised as if he could stop the bullet, but Milo's fate ended before his bowels could release from his flesh.

Boc!

The crowd of men froze in place as Halo moved over to his body and released three more shots into his torso. He turned around to the group of men. Halo put his gun back in his waistline. "Now this is where the easy part comes in. I need half of you to keep this spot moving, and the other half will leave with me to head for Atlanta. After things are settled with God's little queen and his Goddess. The regular routine will start again. Is there any questions?"

The men remained silent. No one damn sure wasn't trying to see a repeat of what just happened to Milo. One man had enough sense to step up and speak, "Uh, I think everybody understands, Halo. Maybe we should just move out and let them follow?"

"That sounds great." He moved past them all, back outside the large home.

After explaining what he wanted done. Halo placed a man in charge of the new territory and took seventeen of Tipton's shooters along with him. Returning Janita's call, he held the phone patiently until she answered on the third ring.

"Yes, Halo?"

"It's done, Goddess. I'm on my way back."

"Good, I'll be waiting for you," Janita replied in a grateful tone.

Hanging up, Halo glanced at the time and placed his phone in the center console. Another mission was down. It was time to handle the business accordingly and finish things in order to see Tipton's mind rest for him to focus on getting home. After regrouping to round up the shoulders. There wasn't any turning back. Even if that meant going to war. There was no more time for slipping or guessing. Halo kept his mind focused on the objective, and that was surely gonna keep him game ready for when the action finally has begun.

Chapter 19
Rogers Federal Holding Facility

Tipton heard the sound of his door flap open and jumped up from his sleep. The sight of his dinner tray hung in the small window forcing him to get out of the bed. After twenty-four hours of being in the box, he still hadn't received his property, hygiene items, nor was he allowed to take a shower. His commissary was held in the bounds of his old cell and the half-decent state trays were the only thing allowing him to get by. He grabbed the plastic plate and pulled it inside, just as Captain Two Fucks placed his head down to view him eye to eye.

"White, I got ahold of your property. I'll have it to you in a minute. I'm hoping you're not having any ill feelings about yesterday, son? It's just the routine for all inmates. You haven't received the piss showers and shit cups slamming through your room at three in morning," he joked with a shady ass laugh.

"Nah, there ain't no problem. I'm just doing my time and preparing to get myself home, sir." Tipton gave him a fake smile.

If only he could've gotten away with beating the old man's ass to death. It was a quick evil thought that he had to quickly shake. The walls were designed for ripping a man's heart out and become a monster. The suction of corruption was unbearable. It was like chemicals suffocating you tighter than a gas mask around your face. It was easy to die by the hands of an inmate or officer. You were limited to certain access, but not much to help you to freedom. It was the way of a black man being incarcerated since the beginning of time.

"Well, that's good to hear son. I'm glad you know about the way I handle things. It shows me I can trust you. I can trust you, can't I White?" he asked with a raised eyebrow flashing the cellphone to Tipton.

"Of course, you can Capt, I don't like to talk period."

"Well, that's great son. You be sure to only call me from underneath that door if it's a major problem." He sat the phone inside the small metal frame and slammed the flap shut.

Tipton stood to his feet, moved quickly and snatched the brand-new touchscreen phone from the small tray window. The power was already on, and Janita's number sat on the screen as if she was waiting for him to call. He pressed the dial button and listened to the service connect his call. T

The line only rung twice before she picked up. "Hey, my King," Janita whispered into the phone as if the call was a secret.

"How did your number get in this cell? And what type of slick moves you making if a captain dropping cellphones off at my door flap?" Tipton smiled from the sound of her voice.

"Because I haven't talked to you in forever. I have my connections, too," Janita bragged.

"Wow, I guess you're like the Queen of magic, huh? I have to admit, you tricked me cause I didn't know what just happened for a second. All I know is I'm getting booked and thrown in solitary. Then I got a racist ass redneck who played the role the entire time." Tipton was standing at the cell door to be sure no one was eavesdropping on his conversation.

"I'm sure trying," her voice seemed to simmer down with that statement.

"Is everything, okay? I know it's hard without me being there, but I would never wanna put you through any stress. That's why I haven't called," he admitted.

"Why didn't you tell me, Peaches, Rex, and Dejuan was on your witness list. These people have been around you for years building a case on you. *All your friends,*" Janita was sure to emphasize her words.

"Yeah, it's kind of a dead issue baby. It's nothing that I can do. All I have to worry about is Sincere coming his ass to my court date. He's a problem and surely gonna be a hazard for me getting home."

"That's a dead issue, baby. It's nothing that he can speak on anymore," she rephrased his line with a serious tone.

"Is that a joke?" Tipton asked knowing that Janita always had a comeback.

"No, it's not Tipton. He's gone, I can't allow anyone to take you away from me. So, I stepped up to handle the business out here until you walk out of those doors. No one is coming to speak against you in court. I can guarantee that shit," she assured.

"That's waddup, ma. I can say that you are my glue with piecing a lot of this together. I'm counting on some extra things to help you guys get Kimmi back. Has he said anything since?" Tipton asked about Rex conniving ass.

"He's picking up his weekly little cash and playing his part like Jason Statham from Transporter."

"I have to get my daughter if that idiot hurts her—" Tipton paused in the middle of his speech to remain humble. "I just have to get her back, Janita."

"I know, baby, I'm going to get her back no matter what it takes. I'm trying my best to deal with everything as it comes. How are you going to handle the other snakes? They're only lingering around while all the nonsense is going. I have Demon, Rika, and Sonya around me twenty-four-seven like you asked me, too. They actually play a major part in fixing this. I know there's only so much you're willing to speak on."

Tipton nodded in approval from his wife's statement. "That's true, to be honest, I just don't want to speak so fast. I never envisioned anything like this happening to us. My mind can't process prison anymore and I damn sure can't picture losing Kimmi like this. I've nearly watched all my close friends and relatives get mixed in the cause of this and lose their lives. I'm tired of death, I'm tired of even dealing. That's the reason I made certain moves out there, so we could always be straight. This shit right here has put a big loophole in making that happen correctly," Tipton admitted.

"I just need you to trust me, baby. Trust that I can make this happen for you. I'm going to get her back because *I'm your wife*. It's my job, not only that, I love your child like she's mine."

There was one thing Tipton didn't want, and that was Janita getting hurt for the mistakes of his actions. That's something he would never be able to forgive himself for. "I just want you to be careful, and always have one of my trusted friends by your side. They'll make sure you're protected at any cost."

"I'm not worried about that, Tipton, because there's been a hell of a lot going since you've left. Still, we're placing things in order as I said. I truly just want you to focus on making it back, Tipton. Come home."

"I will, Janita, I'm coming home. I salute the way you standing up, right now, and just know that your effort means the world to me. I love you."

Janita smiled on the other side of the phone. "Thank you, my King, and I love you, too. It was my mission to make sure you can talk to me. What are you gonna do about, Peaches? You know she played one of the biggest roles in this." Janita asked in case things got out of control.

"Yeah, I figured." He took a deep breath and contemplated it. "Get rid of her ass, too. She's caused too much chaos, she has to go, mandatory. We can speak on that another time." He cut it, not wanting to continue the delicate talk across the line.

"Well, I'll let you get settled. There's a reason you're in solitary confinement. I'll be video chatting you later." Janita giggled lightly.

"I'll be waiting." Tipton grinned before pressing the end button on the cell.

He stared at the device, then began to scroll through it. The finesse of Janita's muscle was surely just flexed. It took some pull on getting anything inside of a federal pin. That showed God's favor for him in some kind of way. It was hard to make great money, become the provider of your own family, and see it all crash to a burning fire before your eyes. There was no hope for Rex because regardless of where he hid. The secret would eventually fall between the cracks.

Only real killers made their mark and threatened to take more just so you know when shit had gotten serious. Tipton was really plugged all through the state of Georgia. Now that the word was out about Rex playing the opposition side. His fate was engraved in stone. The only problem was hunting him down until he gave up all the information they needed.

Tipton wanted to know it all. The new address for his grandma's spot, the last bill he paid, down to the last time he took his last shit. Not only was the routine of studying a nigga balance for any task you were facing, but it scared the shit out of a nigga who knew you were coming specifically for him. That moment when you drew the weapon and took his pathetic ass life. The art of patience, and learning molded you for that. It was the same reason Tipton would smile when he witnessed Rex taking his last slow breath.

Chris Green

Chapter 20
8 Hours Later

Decatur, GA

The sound of *J. Cole's* album *For Your Eyes Only* boomed loudly through Biggs speakers as he drove smoothly down the street in his new white C-Class Mercedes Benz. The foundation of Georgia was about to rise again, and he wanted in. Without the right connections on the streets, you were gonna have to cop a brick for at least twenty-five apiece. That was just a starting rate depending on how good the quality was. Now that the official drought was in. The market was high, and it was time to see some real paper come in. As he turned down into the intersection of his home, the seven black trucks surrounding his crib forced him to slam on the brakes. His mind instantly thought it was a jack move and reached for his gun. The sight of Janita walking towards his whip forced him to second guess. Her tight, black, skinny jeans demanded attention, and the firm peak coat she wore complimented her figure tremendously.

Instead of knocking on his window like a lost desperate woman in need. Janita stopped a few feet from his car window with her hands crossed innocently.

Biggs looked at her curiously before slowly rolling his window down. "Are you lost or something? Any reason all of these cars in my fucking driveway?"

"Hey, I don't mean to intrude, but I'm here on behalf of my husband, Tipton."

"*Tipton?*" Biggs repeated with a suspicious eye. "I don't know what the hell you're here for, but my ears have heard word that Tipton got knocked. I don't know you, so whatever you trying to do is not about to work."

Janita exhaled calmly. "Tipton is handling a case, right now, but this isn't about him. We need your help, and I'm here to negotiate the problem between you and my husband."

Bigg's eyes noticed the men who began to step smoothly out of the trucks in front of him. Their hands were occupied with some shit that could swiss cheese his car within seconds. Their feet never moved towards his vehicle, but their expressions were obviously waiting on a call from the woman standing in front of him.

He cut his eyes back to Janita and frowned. "What is this about?"

"Needing your help, I come in peace. I don't wish to waste any of your time. I know that you have a large team throughout the city. A team that could really assist me with a small problem."

"What the hell are you talking about? What does my men have to do with helping you or Tipton? He has a different crew on every block in Fulton County."

"That's understood, but we're in need of shoulders, not workers. There's a big difference. I'll be clear on what I'm saying so there's no missing gaps. Within a few days, your crew can come assist me with this situation. In return, I'll remove Tipton's hustlers from your corner. The payments will cease, and it'll smooth any ties for future business. I know that you and my husband may have started out on a bad note, but this is where I smooth things out."

"Why do you need my help? What more can my men do, when all these killers you got standing in front of my crib is already prepared to die for you?"

"That's what they're paid to do. A different presence is what I need," Janita corrected him.

"So, basically you want my name to be backing you with a beef that I know nothing about?" Biggs sat back in his seat. "What the hell would make me do that?"

"Because, I had enough guts to ask you, unlike most of the pussies that hide their hands. This is business, not a favor. I never said you had to agree, but I will say that I'm not trying to differ about the same thing. All you have to do is say no."

Biggs could tell by the sound of her comment that she was looking for the right answer, and disagreeing was surely gonna force him to blow her brains out with the Glock .40 handgun that he clutched on. The goons standing across from his whip lurked with anticipation. Their posture was surely shifting by the second.

Before anything spiraled out of control, he buried the hatchet. "What do you expect me to do? Because I'm not crashing out for this man?"

"No crash outs let's just say it will be better for both sides. I'm showing unity and breaking the grip with any misunderstanding. The only way I can agree to that happening is if we work together. Consider it a meeting to ensure that this city is divided correctly. I'll call, your men will show and we all leave satisfied," Janita encouraged.

Biggs mumbled a few words to himself before making the best decision for his crew. "I'll be there just make sure you hold that agreement the same way."

"All I have in this world is my word and my pussy, neither one has ever lied before," Janita smirked and turned to leave.

After giving the men a nod confirming their alliance, she climbed back into her truck and looked over at Sonya with a smile. "It's done."

"What did he say?"

"Exactly what we needed him to."

***

1:38 a.m.

As she sat at the kitchen table of her home, Janita placed the last of her mission in order. The information Demon gave her over the phone earlier concluded that their new route was full proof. After splitting the men into four groups. Janita stationed them in different areas and gave Halo the complete run down. Her trust level with him didn't deflate and give the vibe she felt from everyone else. So, in order to ensure that shit fell accordingly, she forced the rest to relocate until the delicate moment approached.

"I know that things seem uneasy, Goddess, but regardless of how it turns out. I'm riding to the end with you and God. I know what this means to you," Halo informed her with a straight face.

"Thanks, Halo, Tipton has the right to call you a true friend and so do I. There isn't any room for mistakes. So, I just wanna make it count for Tipton."

"Understood. Is that truly what he wants to happen with Peaches as well?"

Janita remembered his words clearly and knew that he wanted her to suffer for the treacherous decision she made regarding their child. The thought of handing Kimmi over to a lunatic for a small payment showed where Peaches' heart stood for Tipton. "I'm gonna handle her personally." Janita nodded.

The loud knock on the front door caused her to jerk around in a quick motion. Halo looked at Janita and motioned his hand for her to stay seated. The loud knock sounded again, removing his pistol, Halo walked over to the front door, opening it swiftly. His mind reacted instantly upon seeing Rex's face on Tipton's doorstep. The pistol in his hand raised within a slight second, ready to pull the trigger. "You must be ready to die, fool? How in the fuck did you find this house?"

Rex held up his hands with a calm attitude. "You know that shooting me will get your little boyfriend's daughter chopped up, Halo. I come in peace. If you don't mind, I would like to speak with the head in charge to discuss business."

Janita's heart pounded harder when she rose from the table to see the devil himself stepping in her living room. Halo aimed his gun with a stiff grip, his blue eyes were glowing with rage, and Janita knew that he wouldn't hesitate to murder Rex if the wrong move was made.

"Halo, no!"

"Listen to the boss lady, sir. You don't wanna do something you might regret," Rex teased knowing that he possessed the upper hand.

Janita stepped in front of Halo, lowered his gun and pointed a stern finger at Rex's face. "Why in the fuck are you in my home? You're crossing boundaries being here."

"I'll say it once again, I come in peace. You said for me to let you know when I made a decision on what's it's gonna be. I made it, now you have to pave it, sweetheart. Calm your little savior behind you down and make him step outside so we can discuss this in private. That's only if you wanna speak business," Rex offered.

"Or how about I murder you and stuff you inside a furnace until I find God's daughter," Halo stressed through clenched jaws.

Rex yawned as if the killer in front of him was so amusing. "Janita, with the push of a button this kid, can be blown away, and you insist on letting this man think so negative. You made an agreement, if you don't mind, tell this Busta to step out so we can handle this issue about Kimmi. That's my last time being willing to negotiate and I mean that" he threatened indirectly.

The question on how Rex found Tipton's home was beyond her mind. The sneaky motherfucker was plotting and looking for an opening to see her weak. He also knew that Kimmi was the biggest factor of all. If Janita pulled a funny move at the moment, it could literally be the last day of Kimmi's life. The thought of Tipton crossed her brain and she used her mind to react instead of her heart.

"Halo, can you step out until I handle this please?" She kept her eyes focused on Rex snake ass while speaking.

"No, Goddess, I'm not leaving you alone with this idiot," Halo bucked, large veins protruded out his forehead just from hearing her ask the question.

Turning to face him, Janita looked deeply into his blue pupils. "We can't take the risk of losing her," she whispered. "I'll be fine, you have to trust me. We don't have a choice. You said that we were riding in this together and that you would listen. I need you to wait on the front porch until I can squash this." Her face pleaded for his compliance.

Halo's lips quivered in anger. Rex was playing with a dark soul, and nothing was worse than sparing the life of a snake who would bite the flesh of his close ones. Tipton's baby girl blocked Halo's cold heart and forced him to slowly walk off. It was hard to oblige with Janita's request, but there was no choice.

As he walked out the front door, Halo looked back at Janita. "I'll be in front of this door until it comes open Goddess." He was eyeing Rex with a bloodthirsty expression before closing it slowly behind him.

Janita remained quiet until Rex started to speak, "I know it's been hard on you lil' mama, but ya gotta blame your husband for this messy ass situation. He was heading for a ditch when he felt it was cool to murder my father. Now it's my turn because his daughter's life will depend on you," he stated calmly walking over to her.

"Make your price, so we can end the small talk please."

Rex shrugged his shoulders and smiled. "I have two demands and if you comply, I'll let you have the kid with no more strings attached, it's your choice."

"I'm still listening." Janita's arms were folded with a blank expression.

"The first request is two-million cash all hundreds. I want every fucking dollar accounted for. This should be done by morning. I'll give you the address to meet me alone. Believe if you pull anything funny, the kid will die in front of you. That's quite simple," he explained.

"And the second?" she asked impatiently.

"Ass." Rex folded his arms with a serious posture.

"What! You gotta have me mistaken for your sister or something. Don't even play yourself, Rex. That's the last warning," Janita's tone sharpened with malice.

"You asked me the price, and I said them draws bitch. See if my demands ain't met, she could easily lose a leg and arm because of you trying to go against my words of peace. I can always make the call, Janita. Just say word, we all can just see how it ends. I can probably guarantee that it's not gonna be your way." He was now inches away from her face with a dirty grin.

"I'm not about to lower my standards because you threaten me, Rex. We can keep this professional, and I'll get you the money." Her expression was growing nervous by the second.

"Now I would like you to be clear on what I offered when he finds out Kimmi is gone. Maybe doing this will teach you not to go against a real man like myself," Rex mumbled with anger.

All that could beat through Janita's mind was being the resolution for Tipton's child to come home. Their life would never be the same if he wasn't able to see the precious face of his little one again. Nothing was worth losing that happiness and love. Before Rex could say another word, she held back her tears and turned around to hold the wall. Her white, satin Sies Marjan dress gripped her bottom allowing his creepy ass to see what she was working with. He moved closer until his manhood pressed against her ass.

Rex leaned down and whispered into her ears delicately, "I'ma show you how a real nigga supposed to dig in that."

Janita could feel his hands slide under the bottom of her dress as he snatched down the white lace panties she wore.

***

Halo paced around the front porch for over fifteen minutes. His mind was telling him that something wasn't right, but Janita's word was final when it came down to the decisions on business. Just when Halo pondered on walking back inside the crib. The sound of the front door opening snagged his attention. Rex stepped out with a trail of sweat rolling down his forehead. A smile was plastered on his face as he strolled past Halo.

"See ya later, hero." He laughed while walking back to his car.

Halo slowly made his way back inside the house and spotted Janita standing in the middle of her living room. It was clear that she had been crying and her arms were crossed with a defeated expression. He rushed over to her and gently grabbed her shoulders. "Are you okay, Goddess? Did he hurt you?"

Janita wiped her face and straightened her posture like a true soldier. "No, the only thing he did was hurt himself. I need you to alert everyone. The exchange for Kimmi is tomorrow, there is no more waiting, this has to end." Janita's hands were fidgeting.

Halo could hear the pain flow from her words. It was the emotions of a woman who was going through desperate measures to ensure that the life of a child was saved. His mind could see what clearly occurred, and for that, he was gonna be sure Rex received a bullet to the head when it all was said and done.

"Whatever you say, Goddess." He pulled his phone out to set things in order with Sonya and Demon.

Janita moved through the hallway and headed swiftly upstairs. When she got to her room, she locked the door and entered Tipton's large bathroom. She turned on the shower, allowed the water to run for a second before stripping out of her dress and climbed in. After the steam started to engulf the glass windows tears erupted from her eyes. The dirty feeling of Rex forcing sex upon her caused Janita's flesh to cringe. She grabbed a bar of soap from the black hygiene holder and began scrubbing thoroughly to remove his filthy scent.

There was only one way to beat a snake-like his ass, that was reverse mind games. The plan she devised was more than perfect, it was full proof. All Janita wanted was Kimmi. The thought of promising her husband about his daughter's safety became a responsibility. Rex's little game of manipulation was about to crumble. Janita was gonna be sure to show him the tricks of monopoly. It was officially his last night rolling the dice.

Chapter 21
The Federal Court: Downtown Atlanta

Agent Witherspoon moved through the courthouse entrance and headed straight for Judge Leazer's chamber on the fourth floor. His mind was in a rage from the recent news on Tipton's case. It didn't take much to break down what was going on and it was clear that the federal case was about to go completely down the drain. Stepping inside of the small office, Agent Witherspoon paused upon seeing Judge Leazer sitting in front of his computer.

"I need a warrant for a search and I mean now." He jumped straight to the point.

"Well, good evening to you too Agent Witherspoon. Is there a reason you're requesting this without giving me a breakdown of what the hell you're talking about?" Leazer questioned. He removed his glasses, giving him a stern look.

"I'm talking about the suspect in your courtroom, Mr. White. He's been incarcerated for a few weeks and now it seems that my key witness has disappeared off the face of the earth. Now, this isn't just a coincidence, and quite frankly I believe that his relatives have something to do with this, sir. This guy is calling shots from a cell," Agent Witherspoon said replied.

Judge Leazer frowned with disbelief. "First off, Witherspoon, you have no proof for your statement. Before you can state an action, you have to bring evidence. Now I'm quite sure there is more to your witness playing the missing role. Are you sure that you didn't have a man who wanted to get off, instead of helping you with your case, because if so, that means this is a personal problem you have on your hands, Agent."

"Your Honor, I've contacted Detective Sandra Elliot and never received a reply. Would you like to know why?"

"I'm sure you're going to tell me anyway."

"It's because she was found dead in her living room this morning, sir. Her face was shredded like a piece of paper and now the police department is looking for answers," Agent Witherspoon clarified.

"Excuse me?" Leazer looked up in surprise.

"Yes, and now we have a bigger problem because all the witnesses for this case has vanished in thin air. I need a warrant to pick up whoever is in contact with, Mr. White, or you're gonna be letting a murderer free at his next court hearing."

Leaning back in his chair, Judge Leazer pondered on his statement. "How can I issue a warrant for a person that isn't involved with the case? It doesn't work that way. You need a witness, son."

"And I have one, all I need is a signature to pick her up," he confirmed.

"May I ask who?"

"Penelope Carter, his child's mother."

Judge Leazer thought before leaning forward in his chair. "Okay, I'm stepping out of the bounds of the law for this. The process is illegal and if you can't produce evidence out of her, she will be no use. You have forty-eight hours to find her if you can't the warrant will be invalid." He grabbed a yellow document from his desk and added his signature.

"Sir, if I don't find her within the next forty-eight hours. I will turn in my badge personally," Agent Witherspoon stated before walking out of his office. There was only one way, Tipton could ever walk away from the case at hand, and that was through his dead body. The thought of Detective Sandra Elliot showed him a different picture of Tipton. One that stated he would do anything for freedom. Even if that meant killing everyone who was involved.

***

Janita pulled her car inside of the bottom of Mozley Park's entrance and shut off her engine. The area was clear of traffic and the sun was shining brightly in the sky. The mission at hand was rattling her nerves, and there was no sight of Rex at the moment. All was in place and Halo was already in position to make sure everyone arrived at the perfect time. Nothing would allow Rex to escape the consequence of his actions. It was surely time to seal the deal of his grimey little games. Janita's eyes roamed the section until she spotted the three cars entering the parking lot behind Tipton's McLaren.

Taking a deep breath, she grabbed the Duffle bags of money and stepped out. Her heart rate increased once Rex protruded from his truck with Kimmi directly by his side. The three-armed men with him showed their weapons to ensure that they were willing to kill if it came down to a sticky situation. At that time, she didn't know if her call would create a disaster, but there was no more space to make excuses. It was no turning around.

Rex smiled at Janita before looking into the bright sky. "This is such a beautiful day. I wonder if it means things are going to work out perfect for us? What do you think, Janita?"

She shrugged her shoulders and smirked. "That's all up to you, Rex. I completed my end of the deal, two-million dollars cash." She sat the large bags down at her feet.

Two of the three men who stood by his side moved forward and retrieved the hefty sacks to inspect the funds inside. Janita looked down at them as they scanned the bills with expertise.

"There's no need to check, it's all there," she assured with a straight face.

Ignoring her remark, one of the shooters looked back at Rex throwing up a thumb.

Janita's eyes never left Kimmi, but she could feel the bullshit approaching from the crooked smile on his face. As the men walked back over to him. He stepped forward. "You know what I respect about you, Janita?"

"No, I don't know and truly I don't care. I handled my end of the deal. Now let her go, Rex," she ordered with authority.

"Hold up, bitch, I'm speaking," he snapped. "Your man has caused a lot of pain in this entire ordeal. I've made a major step by allowing her to be brought back in front of your presence, but something is still missing."

Janita fumbled with her fingers while looking around for her signs of help to appear.

"It seems like I'm still down on my dick with the game mama. See, the only way I can win is if Tipton is dead. That'll make us even." Rex gave her a nasty grin.

"That's not my issue, I'm only here for the baby. She has nothing to do with that." Janita sensed that he was about to try a dirty stunt.

"That's where you're wrong sweet puff." Rex removed his pistol. "Tipton destroyed everything I had. Down to my childhood, even the relationship with my sorry ass Dad. Maybe she deserves the same fate." His eyes looked down at Kimmi wickedly.

"Rex, don't do it!" Janita stepped forward in fear. Her eyes could see his next action approaching.

"Don't what?" Rex's finger pulled the hammer of his gun back. The sound of speeding cars snagged his attention. Jerking his head over to the entrance, he watched a long line of vehicles pull quickly inside of the park's driveway. Rex snatched Kimmi in his arms knowing that the police were obviously brought into the picture. There wasn't gonna be an easy takedown. He was definitely willing to be murdered before grabbing a life sentence off the shelf.

Another row of trucks proceeded through the top entrance one by one. Rex couldn't count the amount but watched as they swarmed through within a matter of seconds. Numerous men began to pour from the vehicles with their guns drawn. It only took a slight blink for Rex to see the barrel of an Ak47 up to his face. Kimmi was snatched from his hands. The pile of soldiers continued to get bigger causing the three men behind him to drop their weapons.

Halo moved like a speeding train through the crowd until he reached Rex. Smashing a hard, right fist into his face, he towered over him with a black SIG Sauer handgun pointing directly at his face. "You know that it's your last day on earth, right?"

Rex shook his head from the heavy blow before spitting out a large glob of blood. "All these niggas, Halo? You really brought all these niggas just for me?" He was now staring around at the forty-plus men who were ready to kill him for any false movement.

Janita rushed over to the man who held Kimmi and wrapped her into a massive hug. Biggs walked smoothly pass her with ten more of his men directly behind him. Giving her a confident wink, Janita nodded. Her cell began to ring at that exact moment. She fumbled to pull it from her pocket, then quickly answered. "Hello?"

"Did it work?" Tipton spoke through the line.

"Yes." Janita exhaled with relief, kissing Kimmi on the forehead.

"Where is he?"

Grabbing Kimmi's hand, Janita moved though the armed men until she reached the front of the crowd. Rex looked up at her with an evil expression. "So, is this what we've come to, Janita? You set me up after I spared your worthless ass life bitch!" Rex shouted with blood spilling from his mouth.

Ignoring his remark, she placed the phone on speaker and put it towards his face.

"I trusted you, bro," Tipton's voice spoke sincerely through the line. "I gave you all I had and brought you around my family, Rex. We were supposed to be fucking bruddas."

Struggling to stand from the concrete, Rex's lips quivered in anger. "You not my fucking brother, nigga. I lost everything, Tipton. You hear me, everything! My childhood was demolished for the sake of your fucking mama. Now I'm sitting here watching you reap all the fucking benefits with no regret." Rex's face was starting to ball up as if he was going to cry.

The large group of men made sure to keep their guns trained as Rex and his three men paced around each other. "Y'all motherfuckers just gotta kill me, because I'm not stopping, Tipton. You know I won't quit!" Rex shouted.

"I'm not worried about you hurting us any longer, Rex. See what you didn't know is that you were figured out from the start. Monopoly is a great game, and you played it well, my nigga. But you missed one thing pussy. I'm the one with the Dopeboy Magic. You're a Federal informant, and I'm quite positive that the people are searching for you, right now. My hands are too sticky to kill you, Rex. You have another purpose. See I slept on you, but there ain't no way to cross a nigga like me without it being exposed. You've been playing under me for years, Rex, but all that ends today."

"The only way it's gonna happen is if you tell ya little boyfriend and clique to do it now, nigga! Tell them to pull the trigger," Rex bucked with venom flying from this tone.

"I don't have, too, because you killed yourself, Rex," Tipton explained calmly.

The sight of five black Mercedes 550s pulled smoothly inside of the park causing silence to fall over everyone. All eyes watched the vehicles until they stopped directly in the center of the chaos. Lotus rose from one of the backseats, and her large group of cartel killers followed closely behind. Her body was wrapped in a black Dolce and Gabbana strap dress. Her red bottom heels clicked gently against the concrete while walking over to the crowded group of shooters who held Rex at gunpoint. Once she reached the front, Janita gave her a stern and thankful nod.

Shaggy's sister smiled with joy. "You guys don't know how much this means to my father, and family. I thank you all for this help. I was glad to be of assistance in getting your baby back safely."

Turning her attention to Rex, she snapped her fingers to four of her guards. Everyone watched them snatch his ass up quickly.

Rex began to struggle in fear. "Who the fuck are y'all niggas man? Get the fuck off me!"

The men held him with ease while standing face to face with Lotus. She looked into his eyes with an unmerciful expression. "I've been looking everywhere for you, sir. You touched the wrong kid and unfortunately, my family is requesting your presence for a personal solution."

"Fuck you, bitch! I ain't scared of shit, I'm already dead hoe." Rex tried to spit on her dress but missed.

One of the strong bulky men caved a hard, fist into his stomach forcing more blood to spill from between his lips.

"He sounds pleased to see us. Take him away." Lotus smiled with excitement. A bag was quickly placed over his head before the men drug him towards one of the parked Mercedes.

Lotus glanced over to Janita and shook her hand. "Thank you for filling me in on this little meet up of yours. I hope we didn't cause too much problems."

"Janita looked down at the bags of money and tapped them lightly with her foot. All your money is here and accounted for. I thank you for supporting Tipton throughout this mess. He sends his gratitude." She held up the phone.

"Greetings, Tipton. Hopefully, we will speak on better terms. Too-da loo, Darling." Lotus strutted off with confidence.

"Hey, what about this?" Janita pointed down at the hefty Duffles.

"Keep it, I'm sure there is some extra things you might need soon. Consider it a gift for my little friend. It was great doing business with you." Lotus tossed the deuces before climbing back into her Mercedes.

Watching the five luxury cars pull out behind each other. Janita glanced over to Halo. He stood in front of Rex's three workers with his gun still prepared to kill. "I got you, Goddess. Just wait in the car," he encouraged her to let him handle the rest.

"I love you, Tipton," she spoke through her cell.

"I love you more, Janita," he replied before ending their successful conversation.

As she picked Kimmi up in her arms, her curious little brown eyes roamed around in fear. Janita could feel her small arms latch on to her neck, and small trembles rumbled from Kimmi's body. Using a hand to cover her ear, Janita carried her over to the truck. Biggs stood on the side with his crew but refused to speak. His grin of respect said enough when she moved past him. The loud gunshots that sounded off next forced Janita and Kimmi to shiver lightly.

Pak! Pak! Pak! Pak! Pak! Pak! Pak! Pak!

There was no need to turn around. The twisted game in Rex's mind had come to an end and Janita ended up with the fucking mystery card. The unknown was always inevitable. Finding all of Rex locations was a small task. The hardest part was getting the coward to bring Kimmi out in the open. Tipton was coaching from behind a wall and Janita mastered the art of his words. Kimmi felt so good in her arms that it didn't seem official until Halo climbed in the driver's seat of her truck.

"I gotta get yall out of here, Goddess. I'll call Sonya and Rika and let them know what you expect."

"Thank you, Halo." She closed her eyes and sat back.

The car began to pull out towards the entrance and the solid team of bodyguards added the extra nine trucks behind them. Halo wasn't hesitating to push the button for their security. The risky shit they pulled to see Kimmi return was deep enough. His honor for Janita rose from the way she handled every step with perfection. Janita said that she was the way on out tricking Rex's conniving ass. Her brain only exposed things that she wanted you to see, but the master moves were under her sleeve like a hand watch. She was the exact replica of Tipton in female form and the dominos surely fell exactly as planned. Sliding out of the entrance, they quickly found Exit 75 and swerved off on the expressway.

Chapter 22

It wasn't over thirty minutes later when Halo parked the car inside of Tipton's driveway. After waiting until their security blocked off the front entrance, he proceeded from the truck and helped Janita and Kimmi out of the backseat.

"Is there something specific you need me to do now, Goddess?" Halo looked at her awaiting their next step.

She held Kimmi in her arms, before staring up at Tipton's home in sorrow. "I wanna move. We can take the money and relocate until we rebuild," Janita confirmed.

"What do you mean rebuild, Goddess?"

"I mean those men we have sitting in front of this home. They placed their lives on the line and I can't just forget that. We have to work if we wanna eat." Janita looked him square in the eye. "Are you with me on this? We still have to see how this turns out for, Tipton. This might have to be our life in order to survive, but I won't drag you if your plans are elsewhere. You don't owe me anything, but I don't feel that I could ever be safe if you or Tipton isn't with me," she admitted.

"My mission is right here, Goddess. I'm prepared to do whatever you need me to." His face showed more loyalty than anyone she'd ever seen around Tipton since they began dating. His spirit made things seem more than okay. He was a piece that she knew Tipton needed to complete his support balance while in the shitty predicament. Halo was a true friend. "Get with Sonya to find a new location for us. You can use Rika connections to help. I'm gonna take care of my business with, Peaches. After she is handled, I'll meet you guys with, Kimmi. Something is telling me that we don't need to be here."

"Understood," Halo spoke while grabbing Kimmi's hand. "Are you sure about doing this? I can handle it if you want me, too," he offered to get rid of any more headaches for them.

"No, this is personal. You can take my car, I'll use the truck to finish this off. I just wanna get it over with so I can move on."

Halo nodded as Janita headed inside the crib. Moving through the front door, she spotted Rika sitting at her kitchen table. "I need you to assist Halo with getting us ready to relocate. You guys are gonna take the baby while I handle this bitch."

"You got her back?" Rika jumped up with a surprised face.

"Yes." Janita folded her arms with a tired expression.

"Oh, my god! Is she okay?"

"Yes, but I don't feel like we're gonna be okay if we don't get the hell away from this house. Halo's waiting on you outside. I have to grab a few things and deal with Peaches before I wrap all this up."

Rika rubbed her temples but listened closely. The chaos for Tipton was slightly over. "So, what does he wants me to do? I guess it's no need for me being around if Tipton's caged behind a wall. The business will go on pause if he's not here."

Janita smacked her teeth before giving Rika a stern frown. "Where the hell you thinking about going if this where the family at? I asked you were we family and you said yes. The business has to go on with or without Tipton. I'm gonna stand behind it with my life if I have too. All you have to do is make the shipments. We're getting it off, making the money and staying under the radar. When Tipton comes home, you won't just be waiting with a reup. You'll have a stern foundation with him. A family bond for holding our loyalty sacred. You have a position all you have to do is play it." Janita tried to boost her coincidence.

"This is the dope game, not a tournament, Janita. What you thinking is easy, could be the same shit that makes you bow down. What makes you think that we can do that without him?" Rika said as if her wild ass imagination was impossible.

"Because I graduated my first round of college with four degrees in business and molding the perfect image for a lucrative setup. This is what I prepared for, and if I would kill my own flesh and blood before it falls on my husband's head. What do you think I'll do if it came down to us surviving? There is no call overriding mine. We stick together until Tipton says otherwise. Do you hear me?"Janita's eyes didn't blink, she was waiting for any sight of doubt in her face.

Instead of bowing down, Rika grabbed her coat and purse from the couch. "I never said there was a call to override you because I don't care what's said or who's in charge. If I'm showing up to do business and lay down support for Tipton. It doesn't have to be scared into me, it's natural for me to follow someone like him. He's a leader. If he married you, the rest shouldn't have to be explained." She opened the front door, then looked back into Janita's face. "I think it's safe to say that you've been handling a lot around here lately. Still, remember the reason you have support." Rika left closing the front door behind her.

Janita felt those strong words sting heavy at her brain. The game either possessed true ones or snakes. So, at the end, it would always still be one decision if she was in the chair to push any buttons. Either you were family or an enemy. The choice was gonna be up to whoever concluded to tread recklessly. Janita moved toward the hallway closet, opened the door and removed the gun from her lower back. Peaches looked up at her in fear. The nappy weave in her head was shriveling from lack of water and her body smelled like a filthy sewer drain.

Janita reached down and pulled the thick tape from her lips. "You know what time it is, right?"

Peaches shook her head repeatedly as if that shit was about to stop something. Her tears were burned out and she was prepared to beg for her life in order to straighten things out. "Please-ee, Janita, I didn't know what else to do. I tried to get her back," she pleaded.

"You brought all this on yourself. Nothing could ever fix that shit and you know it Peaches. If you make me kill you faster than planned, it's your fault." Janita picked up the brown bag and placed it over her head.

She slowly lifted her sour body from the soiled floor. She turned her nose from the scent that blasted through her nostrils. Then she walked her to the door, led her outside, and guided her inside the backseat of the rented Yukon Denali. Being sure to click the child's lock. She closed the door and climbed behind the driver's seat. After starting the engine, Janita pulled out of the lot, listening to Peaches' pleas for mercy. Every other second, she was asking funny shit that didn't mean nothing, especially the conversation that supposed to end with death. The small drive was a little over thirty minutes. Peaches grew quite after a while once she realized there was nothing said since their encounter in the closet. Her movements began to shift when the car came to a screeching halt.

Janita knew that another issue would hinder Tipton, and just the feeling of getting Kimmi back safely, also said that it was some hope in him coming home a lot sooner. In order for that to transpire, all loose ends had to be slashed out. She climbed out of the truck and pulled Peaches from the backseat. She walked a small distance from the vehicle, snatched the bag from her head and removed the zip tie from her swollen wrist.

Peaches looked around the large empty parking lot, before facing Janita. Her pupils rotated down to the gun she was holding. "Please, Janita, I swear I didn't know what he was going to pull with Kimmi. I just need more time and I can get her back." She was holding her hands out like an innocent child running from a mother's leather belt. After sitting in a closet for days with little to survive on, the realization came to her fake ass world that death truly existed. That someone could really remove her life within a second of time. A bullet from Janita's gun wasn't the last vision she wanted to see crumbling her world before she could seek her daughter and Tipton's forgiveness.

"You were the reason all this happened, Peaches." Janita glanced out at the car passing the empty store lot. "This isn't about anyone else, right now. Tipton doesn't expect you to even be alive, right now. Do you realize what the fuck you've caused?"

Peaches panted knowing the next answer could probably get her shot. "I can fix it," she mumbled in fear.

Janita reached for her waist causing Peaches to flinch. The paper ticket and manila envelope she pulled out was folded with a small rubber band bounding it together. She tossed it towards her feet. Peaches shook nervously before looking down at the small package in front of her.

Janita raised the gun before she could utter a word. "That's ten thousand dollars and a bus ticket to another state. The only reason

I'm not following Tipton's request is because I have to look at your daughter for the rest of my life. I refuse to let her hate me for murdering you. I'll be the best mother for her and this is my way of sparing you from my husband's wish Peaches. Take the money and leave. If you're caught anywhere back down in this city. I'll erase you with no regret. The greyhound station is directly behind this area. If you're thinking of doing anything different, I can just end it the way I planned at first." Janita gave her an option with no room for debate.

Peaches fumbled to pick up the envelope and looked up into Janita's eyes. "Can I see Kimmi again? Janita, she's my baby?" She released a few tears of sorrow.

"I'm sorry, but she's my child now. It's either that way or a trip to a casket now, pick one." She placed a bullet in the chamber.

Sucking up the emotions to face her wrongs, Peaches backed slowly away while nodding. "I'll leave, just let me leave. Please!"

"Go!" Janita shouted.

Her loud voice caused Peaches to turn around and run for her life. The way she zooted through the empty lot gave the confirmation that she wouldn't have to ever be seen again. It would have been critical to see Kimmi's mother never speak to the child she birthed again, but her death could have made that even harder to deal with. It was only a good deed to replace a bad one, if Peaches decided to go against that, shit would only crash for the sake of her child, and of course of her own life.

Janita exhaled before jumping back in the truck. After weeks of suffering, she could actually say that it was finally over. She drove out of the parking lot and headed to meet Halo and the rest of their team. There was only one thing left to unfold, that was Tipton's date on seeing how long he would be away from the family's table.

Chris Green

Chapter 23
11 Months Later

Rogers Federal Holding Facility
10.34 a.m.

Tipton smiled as he stepped out of the front doors of the institution. It felt good to finally be home, back to his life. He could see Janita waiting outside of the bob wired fence with a small smile. After a year of being incarcerated. Wallace kept his promise and was sure to make the deal for a year of time served. Agent Witherspoon pushed the issue, but fell short with his lack of witnesses, especially when the people found out about the disappearance of Peaches. The case was either gonna be settled for a year, or Tipton would have surely walked out a free man. The pain and struggle were now over and that day had finally come.

The buzzing from the sliding gate sounded off as Tipton stepped closer. Janita slowly moved towards him with a small frown. Her eyes were soaked with tears and her hands were trembling with joy when he wrapped her into a firm hug. Their lips connected, he savored the taste of her tongue, before looking into her face.

"It's okay, baby, I'm here."

"I missed you, Tipton," she whispered under her breath.

"Baby, why you sad? The hard part is over. Where is Kimmi?" Tipton asked with a huge smile.

Janita's words were caught between her lips. Tipton stared into her eyes, he could sense that she wasn't herself. He grabbed her face gently and glared down at her. "Baby, where is Halo and Kimmi?"

Before she could give her reply. The car door of her Mercedes opened, and Churro stepped out of the front seat. He was dressed in a tailored black suit and a pair of brown dress shoes.

"Churro?" Tipton looked at him confused. "Why the fuck are you getting out of my girl's car? And when in the hell did you get out?"

"Tipton, I know there is a lot you may not understand at this time. I think that we need to go somewhere and have a talk."

"Talk about what?" Tipton placed his attention back on Janita. "What the hell is going on?"

She grabbed his hand holding it tightly, before releasing tears of distress. "They have, Kimmi, baby. They took her and I couldn't stop them." Janita lowered her head in defeat.

"Who has, Kimmi? Janita what are you talking about, baby? Is this a joke?" Tipton's heart rate started to pump faster.

"His name is, Delmeto, Tipton. I know it may be hard to take in right now, but this is the man I work for. He's the same man your mother moved cocaine for years ago. He's requesting to speak with you," Churro explained sincerely.

"What! Churro, where in the fuck is my daughter?" Tipton's lips curled with venom.

Exhaling, his old friend lowered his head. "She's in Cuba."

Tipton moved closer to him with clenched fists. "I think you need to tell me what the fuck is going on before I catch another murder in front of this fucking prison, Churro."

"Hey, man, calm down. I'm not your enemy, Tipton. If I was there would be no reason for me to be standing in front of you. I'm here to see that this is straightened out but coming at me will do you no justice. You need a connect and I mean fast. My boss only wants your business and he's willing to do whatever to get it. Your wife has cut off all your ties in Atlanta, and certain people have backed away from the cause of you being incarcerated by the feds. Nobody wants to deal with you on product, and that's surely what you're gonna need. I've been in Atlanta for weeks trying to help your wife figure this out, but we don't have time to waste. You need someone with a lot of good cocaine, I mean fast," Churro warned with a helpless expression.

Tipton rubbed his head roughly trying to shake the nonsense crawling back into his brain. Nothing could be worse than his baby sliding out of his hands once again. The feeling of her being taken was a flashback to his past with Rex. It was a day that he never wanted to relive again. He gazed at Janita with a clueless face and rubbed her hands. "

Okay, baby, we should be okay. All we have to do is use our connections in Cali and Georgia. We can get whatever we need from them and take care of this," Tipton suggested with worry.

She shook her head disagreeing. "Baby, all the connections have slashed ties. I allowed them to walk away after they helped us the first time. I didn't know what else to do. We're alone," Janita stressed.

Tipton took a small second to soak in his new problem. Looking at the prison behind him, he vowed to never allow the people to take him back through the walls of hell again. Leaving his family placed a hex on them. Now upon his freedom, he was facing a new disaster.

"Give me your phone." Tipton held his hand out to Janita.

She dug into the front pocket of her jeans, removed her cell and placed it into his palm. Tipton quickly dialed a number on the screen. He took a few steps to the side out of ears reach. The line rang in his ear three times before Bigg's voice spoke through the line.

"Yo, who is this?"

"It's me, Tipton." A moment of silence fell through the phone. Tipton could sense his energy about to go left field. "Before you go off the handle. I'm only calling because I need your help."

"Really? It was made clear to me before you caught the little time that we have no more business ties. This was agreed to unless you didn't get the memo. Do you know how hot your name is, right now, fool?" Bigg's voice was stern.

"I understand, and I'm aware of what you and my girl agreed to, but this isn't about me bro. My fuckin' daughter is in trouble. I need help now. I'm asking for your assistance, Biggs, nothing else." Tipton could hear a small huff blow through the receiver.

"What the hell do you want from me man?"

"I need a connect on work asap, a lot of it," Tipton requested while looking back over at Churro and Janita.

"To be honest, bro. I've slowed shit down since you've left. I'm moving different, but it doesn't mean that I can't point you in the right direction. I've been doing business with a new playmaker, but you know if I give you her information, you can't mention me." Biggs threw him the best option possible.

"Who?"

"Tori."

Remembering the woman's name from the recent street buzz, Tipton couldn't help but shake his head. Ever since he left the block dry almost a year ago. Tori was the new name ringing Christmas bells through Atlanta. It was known that she didn't hesitate to create a bloodbath if her way didn't go as planned, but there was no other choice for Tipton. Jumping back around the negativity on meant one thing. The old him would have to resurface.

"I need you to make the call."

"Hold on." Biggs dialed the number through his cell and placed a three-way. Once the phone began to ring, Biggs spoke quickly, "You're on your own now, big dog. I'll be on mute while you talk, cause you know how this chick works."

"I understand," Tipton replied just as she picked up the line.

"Who is this? I don't like private numbers so please speak quick."

"I know this may be a bad time and I'm not properly addressing you. The name is Tipton. You may not remember me, but we have mutual connections. I'm in bad need of your assistance."

"Tipton?" Tori repeated through the phone. "I do remember, but how in the fuck did you get my number?" she questioned suspiciously.

"Maybe I can explain to you better face to face. I'm sure you know what I'm capable of. I promise to make it worth your while. Please," he begged waiting for her response.

"I'll get back with you in twenty-four hours. Please don't miss the call, because I don't like sloppy business, Tipton." She hung up the line in his face.

Blowing some hard steam from his chest, he turned around and made his way back over to Churro and Janita. Locking eyes with his bunkmate, he frowned. "We can go to my place. I want to know whatever the fuck you know. Do you hear me?" Tipton demanded.

"I'll tell you everything from the beginning," Churro agreed as they all climbed inside of the Mercedes to exit the parking lot of the prison.

The deep drama had gotten worse. It was beyond life, it was operations at stake, and Delmeto the devil of Cuba was the man holding the last say so on who won or lost.

To Be Continued...
Dope Boy Magic 4
The Collision of a Dopeboy & Dopegirl
Coming Soon

Submission Guideline

Submit the first three chapters of your completed manuscript to ldpsubmissions@gmail.com, subject line: Your book's title. The manuscript must be in a .doc file and sent as an attachment. Document should be in Times New Roman, double spaced and in size 12 font. Also, provide your synopsis and full contact information. If sending multiple submissions, they must each be in a separate email.

Have a story but no way to send it electronically? You can still submit to LDP/Ca$h Presents. Send in the first three chapters, written or typed, of your completed manuscript to:

LDP: Submissions Dept
Po Box 944
Stockbridge, Ga 30281

DO NOT send original manuscript. Must be a duplicate.

Provide your synopsis and a cover letter containing your full contact information.

Thanks for considering LDP and Ca$h Presents.

Coming Soon from Lock Down Publications/Ca$h Presents

BOW DOWN TO MY GANGSTA
By **Ca$h**
TORN BETWEEN TWO
By **Coffee**
THE STREETS STAINED MY SOUL **II**
By **Marcellus Allen**
BLOOD OF A BOSS **VI**
SHADOWS OF THE GAME II
By **Askari**
LOYAL TO THE GAME **IV**
By **T.J. & Jelissa**
A DOPEBOY'S PRAYER **II**
By **Eddie "Wolf" Lee**
IF LOVING YOU IS WRONG... **III**
By **Jelissa**
TRUE SAVAGE **VII**
MIDNIGHT CARTEL III
DOPE BOY MAGIC IV
By **Chris Green**
BLAST FOR ME **III**
A SAVAGE DOPEBOY III
CUTTHROAT MAFIA II
By **Ghost**
A HUSTLER'S DECEIT III
KILL ZONE **II**
BAE BELONGS TO ME III
By **Aryanna**

CHAINED TO THE STREETS III

By **J-Blunt**

KING OF NEW YORK V

COKE KINGS IV

BORN HEARTLESS IV

By **T.J. Edwards**

GORILLAZ IN THE BAY V

TEARS OF A GANGSTA II

De'Kari

THE STREETS ARE CALLING II

Duquie Wilson

KINGPIN KILLAZ IV

STREET KINGS III

PAID IN BLOOD III

CARTEL KILLAZ IV

DOPE GODS II

Hood Rich

SINS OF A HUSTLA II

ASAD

TRIGGADALE III

Elijah R. Freeman

KINGZ OF THE GAME V

Playa Ray

SLAUGHTER GANG IV

RUTHLESS HEART IV

By **Willie Slaughter**

THE HEART OF A SAVAGE III

By **Jibril Williams**

FUK SHYT II

By Blakk Diamond

THE DOPEMAN'S BODYGAURD II

By Tranay Adams

TRAP GOD II

By Troublesome

YAYO III

A SHOOTER'S AMBITION III

By S. Allen

GHOST MOB

Stilloan Robinson

KINGPIN DREAMS II

By Paper Boi Rari

CREAM

By Yolanda Moore

SON OF A DOPE FIEND II

By Renta

FOREVER GANGSTA II

GLOCKS ON SATIN SHEETS II

By Adrian Dulan

LOYALTY AIN'T PROMISED II

By Keith Williams

THE PRICE YOU PAY FOR LOVE II

DOPE GIRL MAGIC II

By Destiny Skai

TOE TAGZ III

By Ah'Million

CONFESSIONS OF A GANGSTA II

By Nicholas Lock

PAID IN KARMA III

By **Meesha**

I'M NOTHING WITHOUT HIS LOVE II

By Monet Dragun

CAUGHT UP IN THE LIFE II

By Robert Baptiste

NEW TO THE GAME III

By **Malik D. Rice**

LIFE OF A SAVAGE III

By **Romell Tukes**

QUIET MONEY II

By **Trai'Quan**

THE STREETS MADE ME II

By **Larry D. Wright**

THE ULTIMATE SACRIFICE VI

By **Anthony Fields**

THE LIFE OF A HOOD STAR

By Ca$h & Rashia Wilson

Available Now

RESTRAINING ORDER **I & II**

By **CA$H & Coffee**

LOVE KNOWS NO BOUNDARIES **I II & III**

By **Coffee**

RAISED AS A GOON I, II, III & IV

BRED BY THE SLUMS I, II, III

BLAST FOR ME I & II

ROTTEN TO THE CORE I II III

A BRONX TALE I, II, III

DUFFEL BAG CARTEL I II III IV

HEARTLESS GOON I II III IV

A SAVAGE DOPEBOY I II

HEARTLESS GOON I II III

DRUG LORDS I II III

CUTTHROAT MAFIA

By **Ghost**

LAY IT DOWN **I & II**

LAST OF A DYING BREED

BLOOD STAINS OF A SHOTTA I & II III

By **Jamaica**

LOYAL TO THE GAME I II III

LIFE OF SIN I, II III

By **TJ & Jelissa**

BLOODY COMMAS I & II

SKI MASK CARTEL I II & III

KING OF NEW YORK I II,III IV

RISE TO POWER I II III

COKE KINGS I II III

BORN HEARTLESS I II III

By **T.J. Edwards**

IF LOVING HIM IS WRONG…I & II

LOVE ME EVEN WHEN IT HURTS I II III

By **Jelissa**

WHEN THE STREETS CLAP BACK I & II III

THE HEART OF A SAVAGE I II

By **Jibril Williams**

Chris Green

A DISTINGUISHED THUG STOLE MY HEART I II & III

LOVE SHOULDN'T HURT I II III IV

RENEGADE BOYS I II III IV

PAID IN KARMA I II

By **Meesha**

A GANGSTER'S CODE I &, II III

A GANGSTER'S SYN I II III

THE SAVAGE LIFE I II III

CHAINED TO THE STREETS I II

By J-Blunt

PUSH IT TO THE LIMIT

By **Bre' Hayes**

BLOOD OF A BOSS **I, II, III, IV, V**

SHADOWS OF THE GAME

By **Askari**

THE STREETS BLEED MURDER **I, II & III**

THE HEART OF A GANGSTA I II& III

By **Jerry Jackson**

CUM FOR ME I II III IV V

An **LDP Erotica Collaboration**

BRIDE OF A HUSTLA **I II & II**

THE FETTI GIRLS **I, II& III**

CORRUPTED BY A GANGSTA I, II III, IV

BLINDED BY HIS LOVE

THE PRICE YOU PAY FOR LOVE

DOPE GIRL MAGIC

By **Destiny Skai**

WHEN A GOOD GIRL GOES BAD

By **Adrienne**

158

THE COST OF LOYALTY I II III
By Kweli
A GANGSTER'S REVENGE **I II III & IV**
THE BOSS MAN'S DAUGHTERS I II III IV V
A SAVAGE LOVE **I & II**
BAE BELONGS TO ME I II
A HUSTLER'S DECEIT I, II, III
WHAT BAD BITCHES DO I, II, III
SOUL OF A MONSTER I II III
KILL ZONE
By **Aryanna**
A KINGPIN'S AMBITON
A KINGPIN'S AMBITION **II**
I MURDER FOR THE DOUGH
By **Ambitious**
TRUE SAVAGE I II III IV V VI
DOPE BOY MAGIC I, II, III
MIDNIGHT CARTEL I II
By **Chris Green**
A DOPEBOY'S PRAYER
By **Eddie "Wolf" Lee**
THE KING CARTEL **I, II & III**
By **Frank Gresham**
THESE NIGGAS AIN'T LOYAL **I, II & III**
By **Nikki Tee**
GANGSTA SHYT **I II &III**
By **CATO**
THE ULTIMATE BETRAYAL
By **Phoenix**

Chris Green

BOSS'N UP **I , II & III**
By **Royal Nicole**
I LOVE YOU TO DEATH
By Destiny J
I RIDE FOR MY HITTA
I STILL RIDE FOR MY HITTA
By **Misty Holt**
LOVE & CHASIN' PAPER
By **Qay Crockett**
TO DIE IN VAIN
SINS OF A HUSTLA
By **ASAD**
BROOKLYN HUSTLAZ
By **Boogsy Morina**
BROOKLYN ON LOCK I & II
By **Sonovia**
GANGSTA CITY
By **Teddy Duke**
A DRUG KING AND HIS DIAMOND I & II III
A DOPEMAN'S RICHES
HER MAN, MINE'S TOO I, II
CASH MONEY HO'S
By Nicole Goosby
TRAPHOUSE KING **I II & III**
KINGPIN KILLAZ I II III
STREET KINGS I II
PAID IN BLOOD **I II**
CARTEL KILLAZ I II III
DOPE GODS

Dope Boy Magic 3

By **Hood Rich**

LIPSTICK KILLAH **I, II, III**

CRIME OF PASSION I II & III

By **Mimi**

STEADY MOBBN' **I, II, III**

THE STREETS STAINED MY SOUL

By **Marcellus Allen**

WHO SHOT YA **I, II, III**

SON OF A DOPE FIEND

Renta

GORILLAZ IN THE BAY **I II III IV**

TEARS OF A GANGSTA

DE'KARI

TRIGGADALE I II

Elijah R. Freeman

GOD BLESS THE TRAPPERS I, II, III

THESE SCANDALOUS STREETS I, II, III

FEAR MY GANGSTA I, II, III

THESE STREETS DON'T LOVE NOBODY I, II

BURY ME A G I, II, III, IV, V

A GANGSTA'S EMPIRE I, II, III, IV

THE DOPEMAN'S BODYGAURD

Tranay Adams

THE STREETS ARE CALLING

Duquie Wilson

MARRIED TO A BOSS… I II III

By Destiny Skai & Chris Green

KINGZ OF THE GAME I II III IV

Playa Ray

SLAUGHTER GANG I II III

RUTHLESS HEART I II III

By Willie Slaughter

FUK SHYT

By Blakk Diamond

DON'T F#CK WITH MY HEART I II

By Linnea

ADDICTED TO THE DRAMA I II III

By Jamila

YAYO I II

A SHOOTER'S AMBITION I II

By S. Allen

TRAP GOD

By Troublesome

FOREVER GANGSTA

GLOCKS ON SATIN SHEETS

By Adrian Dulan

TOE TAGZ I II

By Ah'Million

KINGPIN DREAMS

By Paper Boi Rari

CONFESSIONS OF A GANGSTA

By Nicholas Lock

I'M NOTHING WITHOUT HIS LOVE

By Monet Dragun

CAUGHT UP IN THE LIFE

By Robert Baptiste

NEW TO THE GAME I II

By **Malik D. Rice**

Life of a Savage I II

By **Romell Tukes**

LOYALTY AIN'T PROMISED

By Keith Williams

Quiet Money

By **Trai'Quan**

THE STREETS MADE ME

By **Larry D. Wright**

THE ULTIMATE SACRIFICE I, II, III, IV, V

By **Anthony Fields**

THE LIFE OF A HOOD STAR

By Ca$h & Rashia Wilson

<u>BOOKS BY LDP'S CEO, CA$H</u>

<u>TRUST IN NO MAN</u>
<u>TRUST IN NO MAN 2</u>
<u>TRUST IN NO MAN 3</u>
<u>BONDED BY BLOOD</u>
<u>SHORTY GOT A THUG</u>
<u>THUGS CRY</u>
<u>THUGS CRY 2</u>
<u>THUGS CRY 3</u>
<u>TRUST NO BITCH</u>
<u>TRUST NO BITCH 2</u>
<u>TRUST NO BITCH 3</u>
<u>TIL MY CASKET DROPS</u>
<u>RESTRAINING ORDER</u>
<u>RESTRAINING ORDER 2</u>
<u>IN LOVE WITH A CONVICT</u>
<u>LIFE OF A HOOD STAR</u>

<u>Coming Soon</u>
BONDED BY BLOOD 2
BOW DOWN TO MY GANGSTA

www.ingramcontent.com/pod-product-compliance
Lightning Source LLC
Chambersburg PA
CBHW060420260626
47161CB00005B/1706